Praise for the
GARY DELANEY SERIES

"Hysterical."
> —*Vic "Each Way" Rizzuto,*
> *professional punter*

"Terrific debut."
> —*Dave Turner, musicologist*

"I'm still laughing."
> —*Bobby Bombolone, bookmaker*

"Surely, there will be a sequel."
> —*Art Deco, top bloke*

"Gary Delaney is my kind of man."
> —*Anita Hardone,*
> *adult entertainer*

DRIVING MISS CRAZY

The GARY DELANEY series

Too Hard Wrong Spot
Great Barrier Grief

Available by emailing martymelbourne@gmail.com
or through Forty South Publishing at fortysouth.com.au

Driving
Miss Crazy

Marty Shevelove

© Marty Shevelove 2024
Paperback: 978-0-9756406-9-2
eBook: 978-17642011-5-5

Published by
Forty South Publishing Pty Ltd
Hobart, Tasmania
fortysouth.com.au

Printed by
IngramSpark

Cover
Alamy stock image BA5MWY

About the Author

With two successful novels under his belt, former journalist Marty Shevelove has taken a stab at short story writing with *Driving Miss Crazy*. The result is a rollicking read, which will be welcomed by fans of *Great Barrier Grief* and *Too Hard Wrong Spot*.

Having left the stifling heat and humidity of Far North Queensland, the rapidly aging author has settled in picturesque northwest Tasmania where he can be found most afternoons stacking firewood and yelling at clouds. He hosts a popular radio show called Rock 'n Rant on Cairns FM 89.1 two afternoons a week and is still looking for that life-changing five-figure quaddie at his local TAB.

The author can be reached via email: martymelbourne@gmail.com

Contents

Driving
Miss Crazy

A s winter took hold and the days got shorter and colder, Nancy Harper's arthritis began to act up. Years of gardening had taken its toll on her back, knees, and hips and on days like today she wondered if having fresh fruit and veggies on the table every day for her husband and three daughters had been worth it. The 72-year-old widow turned up the thermostat in her two-bedroom flat to 22° during the long Tasmanian winter, but the chill still found its way into her brittle bones.

At least she didn't have to worry about her heating bills like some of the women she had lunch and a chat with every Wednesday afternoon at the local church. How to get a fortnightly pension payment to last a full two weeks was usually the main item of conversation. Mavis Fitzsimmons, the only one of the four who hadn't lost her husband, was checking her blood sugar every other day to offset the cost of the glucose test strips she used. Irma Luzinski sometimes went without dinner – although she always made sure her 14-year-old cat was well fed – and Betty Monroe had begun getting into bed and under the covers right after dinner to avoid turning the heater on in her living room.

Financially, Nancy was much better off than her three friends, and luckier too. A year ago, just a week after hitting a pokie machine jackpot at the casino in Launceston for nearly $8000, she gave Mavis, Irma, and

Betty each $1000 cash at a Christmas in July church function. They opened the envelopes, read the cards, and handed the cash back. Women of their generation were too proud to ever accept help or ask for it.

Nancy Harper's husband of 49 years was a wise investor but didn't live long enough to enjoy the dividends from companies like Microsoft and Apple which flowed into their joint account twice a year. A keen litigator, Morris Harper collapsed on the golf course on Melbourne Cup morning two years ago with several TAB tickets in his pockets, all of which turned out to be winners. Nancy kept them instead of cashing them in and last year – her first cup day without her husband – she went to the movies. "Any movie without a horse in it," she told the young girl at the ticket window who asked what film she wanted to see. Nancy didn't find out who won the great race until she picked up a newspaper the next morning.

In addition to her arthritis, Nancy's eyesight had begun to fail. She had worn glasses for the past 20 years but was so far-sighted her GP recommended she give up driving. Nancy was unwilling to give up her independence, so they compromised. She would not drive at night and stick to roads she was familiar with and not venture any further than the local shopping centre just a few kilometres away from home. It included Coles, her bank, the post office, the chemist, a bakery, and The Reject Shop where she occasionally picked up odds and ends. For any other outings, she either called a taxi, depended on her friends and neighbours or her children.

However, Nancy soon tired of asking for rides or calling a taxi, and just six weeks after the visit with her GP, Nancy got behind the wheel of her three-year-old Kia several times after dark. It had so many safety features built into it – beeps which sounded if she got close to any objects, forward collision warning, lane departure warnings, lane keeping assist, blind spot monitoring, rear-cross safety alert – that Nancy was sure she could go to a movie, a concert or even a play put on by the local theatrical society without putting herself or others in any danger. She had once close call and it was while backing out of her narrow driveway in broad daylight. She clipped the edge of her fence and scrapped a bit of paint off the back door on the passenger side which annoyed her to no end.

Nothing happens to me on the roads, but I back out of my own driveway and bang.

A week later she noticed that her left front tire was sitting a little low. *What the fuck is going on here?* she wondered.

Ordinarily Nancy was not one to use foul language. "Fuck, fuck, fuck," she yelled. She put her seatbelt on and then pounded the dashboard. She waited until she cooled off before turning the key. *I don't what's come over me,* she wondered. *I don't usually get this worked up. It's just a flat tyre for goodness' sake. Happens to thousands of people every day.*

Nancy carefully and successfully backed out of her driveway and slowly drove the car to a nearby tyre centre.

"Here's your problem," a young repairman said. "A nail in the tyre."

It was patched up in 10 minutes and after paying the $44 bill, she was on her way.

Nancy's three daughters were scattered in all directions and were so busy with work and ferrying their kids to football and soccer practice, they were only able to visit once every six to eight weeks. The last time the whole family got together was on Christmas day – four months ago.

The change in Nancy Harper's behaviour was the topic of conversation as her daughters and their husbands said their goodbyes after Christmas lunch, the third without Morris at the head of table. Lunch dragged into the early evening. Susan Beveridge, the youngest of the three, was gobsmacked when she heard her mother swear several times and couldn't believe her eyes when her mum lit a cigar after dinner and smoked it.

"Not only that, did you notice how many glasses of scotch she had?" she said to her husband Cal, a builder and part-time potato farmer, on their way home from the gathering.

"I sure did," Cal said. "I counted four, and she didn't seem overly happy to see all the grandkids either."

"I'm a bit worried Cal. You don't think there's anything wrong with her, do you?"

"I don't think so. What was it she said? That they were your dad's cigars and whiskey, and she didn't want them to go to waste? She might be the only widow in northwest Tasmania smoking cigars and drinking scotch, but it's not that out of the ordinary. If she buys a smoking jacket and starts reading Dickens, Joyce, and Jane Austen, and buys a pipe, then I'll start worrying."

"I suppose you are right. But just to be safe, I am going to keep an eye on her."

Since the Beveridges lived less than an hour away from Susan's mum on a seven-acre spread outside Ulverstone in the northwest part of the state, the responsibility of looking after Nancy Harper fell to them by default. Older sister Sharon, her husband and their three kids lived in Melbourne, while middle sister Michelle, who was sure that her husband of a decade was cheating on her, lived in Hobart.

Three weeks after the Christmas Day gathering, Susan Beveridge was driving into town to grab a few things before picking up her young ones from soccer practice. She was waiting for a light to change when a big Harley motorcycle pulled up alongside her. A big, hairy fellow, clad completely in leather, was driving, and seated behind him, with her arms wrapped tightly him, was a woman who looked just like her mum. They made eye contact just as the light changed. The woman waved as the noisy bike sped off. *Was that Mum? Nah. It couldn't be. But it sure looked like her*, Susan Beveridge thought.

Her thoughts were confirmed later that afternoon when she rang her mum.

"That was me alright. I took a ride with one of The Outlaws. It was so cool. I might get me a Harley."

"Tell me you are kidding Mum."

"Of course, I am kidding. But it was fun. Clyde is a lot of fun. I'm going to see him this weekend."

"You're going out with a biker?"

"They're so misunderstood Susan. He's a university professor. You'll have to come over and meet him one day."

"Meet him? Dad's barely been gone a year and you're dating a biker?"

"It's not called dating anymore hun. We call it hooking up."

After dinner that night Susan had a long talk with her husband. "She's sleeping with a biker, Cal. A fucking biker."

Susan Beveridge rarely cursed so Cal knew his wife was angrier than a Collingwood supporter. He decided to let her continue with her rant until she ran out of puff.

"And there is more Cal. She's planning on going skydiving to celebrate her 73rd birthday next month. Where do you suppose she got that idea? "Why couldn't she have taken up golf. Dad's clubs are still in the garage."

Susan finished her glass of wine and then started in again.

"You don't think she is losing her marbles Cal, do you?"

"Not at all. She's just having a little fun while she can. But if it makes you feel better, we'll make an appointment for her to see Dr Fanning."

Cal had another two weeks of work on the site of the local primary school close to where Nancy lived. The school was adding a new building of classrooms to handle its growing enrolment and Cal knocked off a bit early one afternoon to take her to the doctor's.

A week before her 73rd birthday, Nancy Harper and Cal Beveridge were sitting in the waiting room at the local medical centre.

After a short wait, Robert Fanning, her GP of five years, escorted her to his examining room. "You're looking well," he said.

Dr Fanning gave Nancy Harper a complete check-up, asked her several simple questions and was happy with her answers.

Since it had been two years since her last major physical, Dr Fanning tapped out a few lines on his computer, printed out a page and told her to make an appointment for a fasting blood test at reception. "It's all routine Nancy. "We're just going to check your cholesterol levels, kidney and liver function, your blood sugar levels. There's nothing to worry about."

"How'd everything go Mum?" Cal Beveridge asked as they walked to his ute.

"Dr Fanning says I am fine. He wants me to come back next week for a complete blood work-up. Then we'll go over the numbers."

Cal nodded.

Cal took his mother-in-law shopping at Coles and asked what she wanted for tea?

"That's very nice of you Cal, but I have a dinner date."

"You do?"

"With the fellow who is taking me sky diving. He says he wants to go over a couple of things, but I think he just wants to get in my pants."

"You're joking, aren't you?"

"Nope. Look at this photo he sent me."

She handed him her phone. Cal Beveridge did not believe what he was seeing. Some bloke, younger than him, was standing bare-chested in front of a small plane.

"I sent him one of me too."

"You had your top on I hope."

"No. Just a bra. That's what he asked for."

Cal lowered his head and rubbed his eyes.

"Mum, you can't send pictures like that."

"I can't?"

"No. For one you are 72 years old. And who knows what he is going to do with your photo. It can wind up anywhere. It could cause you a lot of embarrassment if it wound up on some inappropriate website."

"What do you mean inappropriate?"

"Don't make me say it Mum."

Despite her arthritis, which got better in the warmer summer months, Nancy Harper was a good-looking woman for someone over 70. At parties and functions she attended with her husband over the years, she had always turned more than a few heads. However, she never cheated on Morris and had only slept with one other man in her life.

"Better start dinner without me," Cal said when he phoned his wife. "Everything is fine. I'm just going to have a talk with Mum. I'll fill you in when I get home."

Despite rides on her uni professor's Harley, her successful birthday sky dive and weekly catch-up with her church friends, Nancy Harper was beginning to get a little restless.

She missed the excitement, the lights, the sounds, and the jackpots at the casino in Launceston, an hour from home. The 20 or 30 machines at a few local pubs, where she never once hit a jackpot, just wouldn't do.

Not being able to drive long distances was the main stumbling block. "How do I get to Launceston and back?" she asked herself. She couldn't ask Susan or Cal. When she told them of her $8000 win, they worried how much she had lost chasing it. She couldn't ask her three church friends either. They had made it quite clear what they thought of throwing good money into a machine.

She decided she would find someone to drive her there in the car which sat in her driveway. Not familiar with Facebook and the online world, she placed an ad in the local paper.

Five days later her ad appeared in print.

Aged lady pensioner who likes to spend the occasional afternoon at the Casino is looking for like-minded persons with licence to drive her car to and from Launceston. Her phone number followed.

"Drive her car? Hmmm. Nobody would ever suspect an old lady of transporting drugs," small-time dealer Willie Mears said when he spotted the ad. Fresh out of jail after an 18-month stint for drug possession, 29-year-old Mears had kept in touch with his mates and now they needed someone to haul a load of methamphetamine from Devonport to Launceston. Using the pensioner's car and having her in the passenger seat would not arouse suspicion. She wanted like-minded persons. *Why not my mum?* Mears thought. *She'd like a day out and doesn't mind having a flutter on the pokies.*

Mears rang the number. "So, you're looking for someone to drive you to the casino?" he asked. "My mum would be happy to do that."

"Tell me a little about your mother young man. I'd like someone who's talkative, has some of the same interests and who's a good driver. Does she have a current licence?" Nancy Harper asked.

Mears gave her the low-down on his mum, Mabel; how she liked to play the pokies (true), that her licence was current (true), that she hadn't ever had an accident or received a speeding ticket (lie), that she liked a laugh (true), didn't smoke (lie), was a regular church goer (lie) and a former hospital nurse (true). Mears didn't tell Nancy his mum got fired for stealing pain killers which he later sold on the street.

"She sounds like she's good company. I would like to meet her first. We can have a coffee somewhere. Would that be, okay?"

"It sure would. "You tell me which day is good for you and she will be there," Mears answered.

Nancy Harper received two other calls regarding her ad before she met Mabel Mears three days later for a late morning coffee at a local cafe.

Both callers were men. The first coughed and wheezed throughout their conversation which put her off right away and the second wanted to spend the night with her at the casino. She politely told the 82-year-old she wasn't interested.

Nancy was impressed with Mabel Mears. She was smartly dressed, eight years younger, a good storyteller and had a good laugh. They were also on the same page politically. "I've voted Labor my whole life," Mabel Mears said.

"Would you be free next week to drive me to and from the casino?" Nancy asked Mabel.

"Now that I'm retired, I have nothing but free time. Thursday though is my lawn bowls day. We play inside now that the weather has turned."

"Let's make it next Tuesday then. We'll leave about 10. We can have lunch together if you like and head for home about 3. Is that okay?"

"Sounds like a good day out Nancy."

Mabel gave Nancy her number in case there was a change in plans and told her she'd be at her place around 10am on Tuesday.

Willie Mears met with his mother over the weekend and told her how things would go down on the Tuesday. "I'll drive you to the old bag's home. Ask her for her keys. Tell her you want to put your bag in her car, so you don't forget it. Do that, pop the boot, and then go inside. I'll have the 50 kilos of meth packed in two boxes and will quickly transfer them from our car to her boot and then take off. When you get to the casino, lock the car but leave the boot ajar. The boys will be watching for her car. They'll move the stuff into their car, close Nancy's boot and then take off. There's no risk unless you speed or run a light so be careful, okay? We'll be paid the next day."

Mabel Mears nodded.

Everything went according to plan on Tuesday except at the pokie machines where Nancy Harper dropped $200 before lunch. As she was eating, her daughter Susan rang. Nancy answered which was a mistake, On the other end of the line the sound of pokie machines and a busy cafeteria rattled Susan. "What's all that noise? Where are you Mum?" Susan Beveridge asked.

"At the casino."

"The casino? How did you get there? You're not supposed to drive on the highway with your eyesight."

"Calm down sweetie. I had a friend drive me. No. Not on the Harley. We took my car. She's nice too. Her name? Um. Mabel. That's it. Mabel Mears."

Mears, that name sounds familiar, Susan thought. "Call me when you get home, okay Mum?"

"I will dear. But there's no need to worry. She's an excellent driver. Bye."

The afternoon wasn't much kinder to Nancy Harper. All up she lost $450. And when Nancy Harper lost, she was not good company. "Those damn machines. They rig them so us pensioners can't win," she told Mabel Mears on the drive home. Mabel nodded in agreement even though she had won $52. And when Mabel Mears won, she liked to celebrate by having a couple of drinks, and then a couple of more. By the time they left the casino and got on the Bass Highway back to Devonport, Mabel was over the 0.5 limit. She was also driving a tad rapidly and doing more weaving than a member of the Launceston Knitting Club.

It was a passing truckie who notified police of a late model white Kia being driven erratically on the west-bound lanes of the Bass Highway.

Less than five minutes later, a police car found Nancy Harper's Kia and pulled up behind it with its lights and siren on. A booming voice from a speaker told the Kia's occupants to pull over onto the shoulder. Mabel Mears took a glance in her rear-view mirror and sped up. Just as she did another police car joined in the chase. Nancy Harper finally realised what was going on, stopped ranting about her loss at the casino and told Mabel Mears to pull over. Police slowly approached the vehicle with their guns drawn and were a bit surprised when they got a good look at the occupants. "Maybe they're escapees from a nursing home. Did you watch *Four Corners* last night? They get treated like shit," Junior Constable Eric Rogers said.

Senior Constable Rick Segretti told his partner to pipe down. "Who knows what we have here."

Segretti tapped on the driver's side window and motioned for the driver to slowly exit the vehicle with her hands help up. Rogers did the same on the passenger side.

"Have a bit to drink at lunch grandma?" Rogers asked Mabel Mears when both occupants had left the vehicle.

"I want you to breathe into this breathalyser ma'am," Segretti asked Mears.

She did as she was told. "One point two five. We have a winner," Rogers said.

"How much have you had to drink today ma'am?" Segretti asked.

"I had a few bourbon and cokes to celebrate. That ain't against the law, is it?"

"Celebrate? You won on the machines?" Nancy Harper asked. "How much?"

"Fifty bucks."

"Didn't you realise your friend here was driving erratically and speeding?" Segretti asked Nancy.

"I didn't. Those machines cheated me," she said. "I want my money back."

"Oh boy," Junior Constable Rogers said while Senior Constable Segretti first checked and then ran Mabel Mears's licence on their patrol car's laptop. Mears had a stack of unpaid fines, an arrest and conviction for theft and two previous DUIs. "Shit, we're going to have to take her in," Segretti said.

While Mears was being handcuffed, Rogers was checking Nancy Harper's licence. "Is this your vehicle?" he asked.

"It is."

"And why was your friend driving and not you?"

"I'm not allowed to drive at night, so she drove me to the casino. I like playing the pokies but they're rigged," she said.

"But it's the middle of the afternoon."

"So, it is."

"Have you had anything to drink today ma'am?" Rogers asked.

"Just coffee with my lunch and some water."

Junior constable Rogers adjusted his cap and thought things over. *We can't let her get back on the road by herself. Maybe she has family nearby. They can come down here pick her up and drive her car home.*

He looked at Nancy Harper, who seemed a bit bewildered. "Where are you taking Mabel?" she asked.

"We've had to arrest her Miss Harper. She was driving under the influence and has several unpaid fines."

"How am I going to get home?" she asked.

"Do you have family we can call?"

"My son-in-law Cal," she said, handing Junior Constable Rogers her phone.

Rogers went through her contact list, found Cal's name, rang, and filled him in on what was happening.

"She's where? On the Bass Highway 30ks outside Launceston? Jesus Christ," he said.

"She's not thinking straight," Rogers told Cal Beveridge. "Instead of upsetting her and having her car towed, I'll drive it and your mother-in-law to Westbury which is about 2k away. Can you have someone drive you to the Westbury Police station and pick her and her car up?"

"Yup. I'm about to knock off work anyways. Give me an hour, okay?"

Cal Beveridge put his tools away and asked apprentice Jackson Billson if he could give him a lift to Westbury. "It's my mother-in-law. She's in a little bit of strife. I don't know what's going on. We'll take my ute. When we get there, I'll drive her car back home. You follow us, then we'll go get your car."

Beveridge decided it was better not to tell his wife Susan what was going on until he saw her later. He did however send her a text message saying he was stopping by Mum's after work and would be home later than usual.

By the time Beveridge and Billson returned to Devonport, dropped off Nancy – Beveridge took the keys to Nancy's car with him – and retrieved Billson's car, it was nearly 6pm and dark. Nearly an hour later Beveridge hugged his kids and sat down to a late dinner with his wife.

"Arrested? What happened Cal? I rang Mum and she told me she was at the casino."

"She was."

Cal then told his wife the whole story. How her mum put an ad in the paper asking for someone to drive her to the casino, how she and Mabel Mears were pulled over police near Westbury and Mabel's arrest for drink driving.

"Doesn't this Mabel have a son who has been in and out of prison?"

"She does although as far as I know he had nothing to do with this."

"Oh my God."

"Mum is fine. I took her car keys so for now she's effectively grounded. We'll have to reassess things."

"What are we going to do Cal? I don't know if she can stay at home by herself anymore. First the biker, then the sky diver and now the trip to the casino. You don't think she's starting to lose her marbles, do you?"

"I'm not sure hun. But from what I saw today, I think she needs some supervision. It might be time to start looking at assisted living places."

Cal and Sue had a long chat with Nancy one afternoon. When the words assisted living were mentioned, Nancy didn't want to hear another word about it.

"I'm perfectly capable of looking after myself," Nancy said angrily.

"Mum, we spoke to Dr Fanning, and he agrees that an assisted living centre would be best for you."

"He does?"

"Yes Mum."

"Will I have my own apartment and be free to come and go as I please?"

"Yes Mum," Cal and Sue said in unison.

Nancy lowered her head and said, "I've always trusted Dr Fanning and I suppose I could try it. But if I don't like the place, can I come back home?"

"Of course you can," Sue lied.

Six weeks later Nancy Harper's unit was put on the market, and she moved into a nearby assisted living centre. The impending sale of her unit would pay for her care at Estuary Acres. She had her own apartment, complete with a small kitchen and a modern bathroom. Nurses made sure she took her newly prescribed medication every day. Residents received three meals a day and there was plenty of fresh fruit available to nosh on between meals. Every hour of the day was filled with activities for the residents. There were card games, bingo, trivia contests, a book club, a pool table and even a putting green. Most nights a movie was shown on a massive TV in the recreation room. Nancy made a lot of new friends and told her three daughters and her favourite son-in-law she was enjoying her new home.

But every so often she got restless. Morning bingo games were fun but not as much fun as sitting in front of a pokie machine.

"I hear you have a car," she said to Irv Rosenstein one afternoon after lunch. Irv was a widower and pushing 80 but still flirted with every nurse he saw and any female resident who wasn't chained to a walker.

Word around the nurse's station was that Irv was selling Viagra tablets to any male resident with a pulse.

Several times over the past month Irv had asked Nancy back to his room but was politely turned down. "Damn," he said after the last time she said no. "I've got to remember to keep my teeth in when talking to a pretty lady."

Nancy Harper sat down on the couch Irv was sitting on and leaned over. She showed just enough cleavage to momentarily stop Irv's heart.

"Fancy a trip?" she asked.

The Older Lady

’m standing outside an airport taxi rank with my winter jacket draped over the handle of my well-travelled suitcase. It's 27° and sunny on the Gold Coast, a sharp and welcome change from the bitterly cold four-degree morning I woke up to in Melbourne.

I'm on a week's holiday by my lonesome and what better place to thaw out than the Gold Coast. I'm not planning on going to any of the area's theme parks. They're for 10-year-olds not 52-year-old single men. On my agenda are sleep-ins, reading by the pool, perhaps a dip in the surf, nice meals, a visit to the casino and a day at the races. One thing I won't be doing is going to see the Gold Coast Suns take on North Melbourne on Saturday afternoon at Metricon Stadium or whatever it's called now. They'll be lucky to have 8000 people show up. I have a feeling that if I rang the stadium to ask what time the game starts, they'd ask what time I could be there. The AFL sure fucked that one up. Had it placed a team in Tassie it would be playing in front of sold-out crowds every weekend.

To get everyone from the airport to their holiday destinations quickly and efficiently, a tanned and pleasant woman in an orange safety vest is asking the 20 or 30 of us waiting for taxis where we're going and then pairing us off. Four people going to Coolangatta are in one group, another six bound for Surfers Paradise were grouped together as were three headed for Southport. I'm one of just two people going to Broadbeach. The other is a woman who I am guessing is in her late 60s. She's tall, slim, very-well dressed and has two smart pieces of luggage, one standing on either side of her. A lime-coloured ribbon hangs off each handle. My suitcase looks like an old cardboard box compared to hers. She looks a bit like Quentin Bryce, the former Governor-General of Australia. We're standing under a shade cloth to avoid the strong sun as we wait for our taxi.

"It sure is nicer here than in Melbourne. On holiday?" I ask. She looks around, thinking the comment is meant for someone else before realising she's the one I am addressing. "I am," she says. "I'm staying at my winter apartment in Broadbeach. It overlooks the surf."

From what I've seen online, my motel room overlooks a parking lot and a pool. And yes, I've been assured it has water in it.

She has a very official sounding voice, like a politician's or a professor.

"And you? Are you here on business?"

"No. I'm on holiday. I always try and get away from Melbourne in July or August for a week."

She looks at me as if trying to figure out what I do.

"I'm a journalist. Gary Delaney," I say extending my hand.

"A journalist, eh? You don't work for that trashy tabloid down there, do you?"

"No, I don't. I work for a racing newspaper."

She finally shakes my hand. "Juliette Gardner," she says, quickly withdrawing her hand.

"You cover the horses?"

"You can say that. I'm often at the races on a Saturday."

That's interesting. I used to own horses with my late husband."

"Any I would know?"

"Probably not. We never won any big races in town although we sure tried."

Just then a taxi pulls up right in front of us. The driver gets out and greets us. "Both heading to Broadbeach?"

"We are," I say.

He takes Juliette Gardner's bags and gently places them in the boot. I toss my suitcase and carry-on bag next to hers. The driver shuts the boot and motions for us to hop in.

Juliette and I climb into the back seat and buckle up.

"I'll drop you off first ma'am. It's easier," the driver says. I look at his name on his licence which is slapped onto the dashboard; It's one I don't have to sound out phonetically. Sam Howard, it reads. I'm guessing he's about 60.

"How do you folks like the sunshine? It's like this every day, that's why I left Melbourne," he says.

"I hope it stays like this all week," I say.

"It's supposed to," Sam Howard replies.

Juliette did not say a word while Sam and I made small talk. Ten minutes later we pulled into the circular driveway of one of those luxury 50-storey buildings on the beach. On my meagre salary the only thing I'd be able to rent at this place is a storeroom, that is if a bank approved my mortgage application. Remembering my manners, I get out of the car first and open the door for Mrs Gardner and escort her to the footpath.

I go back to the cab and help Sam with Juliette's bags and take mine and put them into the back seat, so he doesn't have to get out of the car when we get to my motel.

"You could have a lot of fun with her," Sam Howard tells me, poking his elbow into my ribs.

"You think?"

"Yup. The older women living in these buildings are not only rich, they're lonely. And you got to admit, she's not a bad looking woman for someone her age."

I glanced back at Juliette as Sam carried her bags straight to the elevator. Sam was right. Juliette must have been a stunner back in her day. She has a pair of long legs partially hidden by a sharp beige business suit. She's from a day when people dressed up when they travelled instead of putting on an old pair of sweatpants, which is what half the people on our flight were wearing.

"Mr Delaney," she called out. She motioned for me to come to the kerb. "Do you know where the Broadbeach Surf Living Club is?"

I didn't, but how hard could it be to find?

"I do, it's just a few blocks from here," I guessed.

"Would you like to join me for tea this evening? Say about six?"

I was surprised by the offer and decided to take her up on it. What else was I going to do? It was no fun eating alone in a restaurant, whether it be in Broadbeach or the Chinese place I frequented often in Melbourne.

"I'd be delighted Mrs Gardner."

"Call me Juliette please," she said. "I'll make a reservation for 6pm under my name."

"Six o'clock it is. See you then Juliette."

She winked at me, or maybe she had something in her eye, or her contacts were giving her trouble. It was one of the three.

A doorman escorted her into the building and to the elevator where Sam had placed her bags. She opened her purse and handed Sam a couple of notes.

"Alright," Sam said climbing back in his cab. "Let's get you to your motel. It's not far. And don't worry about the fare. Your lady friend paid it and gave me a nice tip too."

"That was generous of her."

I was going to tell Sam about my dinner plans but decided against it. He dropped me off at my motel and went straight back to the airport to wait for the next incoming flight full of frozen Melburnians.

For a three-and-a-half star joint my home for the next week was better than I expected. It was clean, bright, had plenty of closet space and a new flat screen TV. The grounds were nicely landscaped, and the pool was in good nick. I looked it over and picked the spot where I would sit the next afternoon; away from the shallow end and the noise of several kids who were still carrying on strong despite a full day at one of the area's theme parks.

It was nearly 4pm when I got back from my brief walkabout and unpacked. I turned on Racing.com to catch the last couple of races from Bendigo, glanced at the brochures I picked up at reception when I checked in, showered and changed into the best clothes I brought with me, pants and shirt from Target, shoes from Rivers. I didn't look too bad for a bloke on the other side of 50 but wondered if I should have brought a sport jacket with me. Who would wear a sport jacket to a Surf Life Saving Club? I asked myself. It's not like I have a yacht moored offshore.

I decided what I was wearing was fine and at 5:30, with my phone showing me the way, I walked to the Surf Living Club. It was a 10-minute walk, and it took me past numerous restaurants, bars, upscale shops and the occasional convenience store.

I told the hostess who greeted me at the Surf Life Saving Club that I had a reservation under the name of Gardner. She found it on a large sheet of paper placed on a lectern in front of her and crossed the name off.

"I'll show you to your table sir," she said. "Follow me." We passed the gaming area, the TAB, a couple of bars and a dining area on our way to the second level. The place was like a mini-Las Vegas. The table was situated on the second level and overlooked the surf. The view was magnificent.

I took my seat at 5:50. At 6pm there was no sign of Juliette. I ordered a beer from the bar. Fifteen minutes later the only company I had was the beer. Watching the waves roll in illuminated by a full moon was not the worst way to pass the time. Several couples could be seen on the sand, sitting on picnic blankets sipping what I guessed was wine. However, when I next looked at my watch and saw that it was 6:32 I wondered if I was being stood up.

She asks me out to dinner and doesn't show? What am I missing here? I wondered. *Maybe she decided to stay in, nodded off and landed face first in a bowl of soup.*

It turned out I wasn't too far off the mark.

Finally, at 20 minutes to seven, I saw Juliette approach the table. I rose to greet her and pulled out her chair. She was wearing a colourful dress, had a beige sweater draped over her shoulders and carried a small purse in her right hand. She was wearing more jewellery than my ex-wife owned.

"I am so sorry Mr Delaney, I took a nap and overslept. If I had your number, I would have rung you."

"That's quite alright Juliette. And please call me Gary."

She nodded and mouthed the words I will.

It had been a long day for us both; getting to the airport, the flight itself, settling in.

"Feeling refreshed?"

"I am. Isn't this a lovely spot?" she asked. "I love sitting up here watching the waves come in."

"What sort of a view do you have from your apartment?" I asked.

"The balcony faces the water, but I am on the 22nd floor. This is much better. The waves are practically on top of us."

After a little more chit chat – the balmy weather, how my accommodation was – we looked at the menus left on the table and decided to order. I had earlier seen a waitress deliver a couple of massive parmas to a nearby table and decided then and there that's what I would have. Juliette ordered a pasta dish.

"Would you like anything to drink? I asked.

"A glass of red please."

"Be right back," I said.

Before I even turned to leave the table, Juliette grabbed my hand and shoved a bank card in it. "Not a word. I invited you."

"Alright."

"Just tap the bloody thing. And get me the best red they have, not the house poison."

Over dinner she told me a bit about herself, how she taught school for many years until she retired just a few years ago. She had planned to spend her retirement travelling around Australia with her husband Daryl, a very successful stockbroker, but he passed away one night in his sleep four years ago, just two months before he turned 70.

"We were married for 41 years," she said. "He was such a good man and so easy to get along with. The only time we really argued was after our infant daughter passed away. He wanted to have another child right away, but I wasn't over the loss of Beth. After that, well ..."

She didn't finish the sentence and took a tissue from her handbag to wipe away a few tears.

Over dessert and coffee – we split an enormous serving of sticky date pudding – she told me how she and Daryl were unable to have any more children. But instead of drifting apart, they grew closer. Apparently, they were friends with some of Melbourne's elite. There were gallery openings, dinners at fancy restaurants and nights spent at the opera and theatre instead of reading night-time stories and putting children to bed. They were members of the Victoria and Melbourne Racing Clubs and never missed a day of socialising at the spring racing carnival.

I processed all the information and figured Juliette was in her late 60s or early 70s. If that was the case, she looked a decade younger.

It was close to 8:30 when we got up from our table. Even at that hour people were still ordering dinner. Outside we breathed in the warm evening air which was a nice change from the cool air conditioning inside.

Now what, I wondered. *Do we say goodnight and go our separate ways? Do I invite her for a drink somewhere?* It was an awkward few minutes until she said she would take a taxi back to her building. I was surprised a driver wasn't waiting for her.

"Thank you for a lovely evening Gary," she said as a taxi pulled up. "It's the first time I've been out on a date with a man other than Daryl in almost 50 years."

"I'm glad you had a nice time Juliette. Thank you for dinner. It was fun."

"What are you doing over the next few days?" she asked as she got into her cab.

"I was going to hang around the pool tomorrow after lunch and I'm definitely going to the races on Saturday. I've never been to the Gold Coast track."

"Why don't you use the pool at my building instead?" she asked. "I'll make lunch for us."

"That sounds nice. I'll be there about noon."

She stopped me from closing the cab door once she was seated. "Aren't you going to kiss me goodnight?" she asked.

I leaned into the back seat of the cab and kissed her softly on the lips, closed the cab door and off she went.

I walked back to my motel, just one of several hundred people walking off their dinners, and stopped for an ice cream. There must have been 20 people of all ages on line in front of me. It gave me a bit of time to think. She's straightforward and says what's on her mind. I'll let her decide what happens next. I seriously doubted we'd wind up in bed together. As I thought about what it might be like I was brought back to reality by a young woman behind a long freezer filled with tubs of ice cream who asked me what I wanted.

"A vanilla cone. Make it a double please, with sprinkles. I'm on holiday."

I paid the $7.50, grabbed an extra napkin off the counter and sat in one of several white plastic chairs on the footpath outside the shop. I finished the cone without any of it dripping on my shirt, unlike a young lad sitting at an adjacent table with his family. His mouth and face were covered in chocolate sauce as was part of his t-shirt. His mum and dad let him enjoy his after-dinner treat instead of reprimanding him. I would have done the same thing.

The next morning, I had a read of the two local Murdoch papers which nearly made me lose the breakfast I had an hour before at a cafe a block away from my motel. Pure celebrity driven tabloid trash although the sport and racing pages were decent. I stuffed both papers – minus the racing pages – in the trash can by the pool where I had planted myself. It was a perfect day, sunny with a few high clouds and a light breeze. It was 21 at 11am which was welcomed by my cold Melbourne bones. A top of 27 was expected.

Juliette's apartment building was a 10-minute walk from my motel. I changed into a pair of board shorts, a short-sleeved shirt, and a pair of boat shoes – thank you Rivers – and with a small bottle of water in my back pocket and a baseball cap on my head left just before noon. I took a right-hand turn and walked two blocks until I came to Broadbeach Boulevard. The ocean was straight ahead. I took a sip of water and breathed in the ocean air for a few minutes. I headed south on Broadbeach Boulevard and five minutes later arrived at Juliette's building, a massive structure just a stone's throw away from the wide beach. I told the doorman, immaculately dressed in a navy-blue blazer and tan chinos, that I had a lunch appointment with Juliette Gardner.

"Ah yes, she's expecting you. Take the elevator behind me to the 22nd floor and then a left. Her apartment is number seven."

I thanked him and was whisked to the 22nd floor in the blink of an eye. It was so fast that my ears nearly popped from the sudden rise in altitude. I rang the bell of 2207 and waited for the door to be opened. Nothing. Zip, Nada. Bupkus. I rang the bell again. Finally, the door opened. I was asked in, but not by Juliette Gardner. A very attractive young woman, clad in an apron with the words "number one chef" printed on it, told me to wait in the large and spacious living area. Her dark hair was pulled back away from her tanned face. She had an oven mitt tucked into the pocket of the apron and held a spatula in her right hand.

"Miss Juliette is coming soon," she said. She bowed slightly and walked back into the kitchen.

She's serving a catered lunch? I would have been happy with a ham and cheese sandwich, I said to myself.

I had a look around the living area while I waited for Juliette. A large and colourful painting of a country landscape hung on a wall above a cream-coloured couch as big as a king-sized bed. A huge television was affixed to another wall. Two very comfortable looking leather recliners were in front of the TV. A large ceiling fan circulated the ocean air blowing through the balcony's open screen door. I stepped onto the balcony and admired the spectacular view. An outdoor dining set and a barbecue took up three-quarters of the space. In the left corner was a telescope pointed to the sky. It would have had terrific views of the night-time skies or views of the lovelies on the beach depending on one's definition of heavenly bodies. I guessed the telescope must have belonged to the late Mr Gardiner. My curiosity got the better of me and I had a look through the telescope at the moon which was still in the sky.

"You're looking at the sky? I'm surprised. I thought you would have had it trained on the girls on the beach the way Daryl used to."

I was a bit startled by Juliette's voice. I laughed off her remark.

"Quite a set-up you have here," I said.

"It's home. Would you like to see the rest of the apartment?"

"Sure."

Juliette turned towards the kitchen and politely asked her house-keeper/cook to place two large glasses of lemonade on the balcony table.

I got a quick tour of the apartment which featured two large bed-rooms, two bathrooms and a study. A family of eight could live here comfortably. Nine if you counted the cook/housekeeper.

After Juliette showed me the apartment, which I conservatively guessed was worth $850,000, we went to the balcony and sat around the table with our drinks. Juliette was wearing a white beach sarong over her one-piece turquoise coloured swimsuit, and I had to say the views the late Mr Gardner had of the heavens could not have measured up to what I was looking at.

This woman is in her 60s? Impossible. She's got the legs of a dancer and the figure a 30-year-old would pay to have.

We made some small talk about the previous evening and the nice weather before I asked about her cook/housekeeper.

"Roberta always gives me a hand when I arrive and looks after the place when I'm in Melbourne. She's a very, very good cook so I have her come over every couple of days to fix my meals. Do you like risotto? That's what we're having for lunch. Chicken and mushroom risotto."

"I love a good risotto. It smells delicious," I lied.

"You've never had it? Have you?"

"No. But I am sure I'll love it."

To tell you the truth it wasn't half bad. It would never be my first choice, but it was okay.

"I guess we'll have to wait 30 minutes before we go for a swim," I joked after Roberta had taken the dishes off the table and refilled our glasses.

"That's what spas are for Gary. The one on the roof is a beauty. It's got jets everywhere and the water is as hot as a summer's day. Let me grab my bag and we'll be on our way. We can get drinks from the bar upstairs."

There's a bar on the roof? This I must see.

Juliette tossed me a large beach towel when she appeared back in the lounge room. "They've got towels up there but mine are better," she said.

She said goodbye to Roberta and off we went.

We got into the elevator and shot up to the 50th floor in a heartbeat. Neil Armstrong and his fellow pilots could have used an elevator like this to simulate launch conditions.

I stepped out of the elevator and into Palm Springs. There were palm trees everywhere and plenty of lounge chairs placed around the 25-metre pool. The spa could have comfortably accompanied 10. Sinatra and Dean Martin would have been at home here, seated at the bar knocking back a couple of margaritas, cigarettes dangling from their lips, gazing at women sunning themselves.

Roberta placed a hat on her head to shield herself from the strong midday sun. I put on my baseball cap. "What's that?" she asked pointing to my head.

"It's my lucky baseball cap."

"You're not going to get lucky here wearing that rag. I'll get you a real hat next time we're out," Juliette said. She was much feisty and livelier than the previous night. A good night's sleep had brought out the real Juliette which I didn't mind one bit.

We slipped into the warm water of the spa, and I reckon I could have stayed there the rest of my life. A bartender brought us a couple of gin and tonics in plastic glasses which she signed for. A few more followed after we swam a few laps and settled into the lounge chairs in the shade of the palm trees. *How good is this?* I thought. *Sure is better than that water-filled ditch back at the motel.*

Roberta had left by the we got back to Juliette's apartment couple of hours later. The place smelled like an Italian restaurant.

"Since you enjoyed your chicken parma so much last night I asked Roberta to make a couple."

"That is very, very sweet of you," I said. "Thank you."

I gave Juliette a kiss and before you knew it, we had tossed off our damp swimsuits and were rolling around in her massive bed. I was barely able to keep up with her. It was like being in bed with a 25-year-old. She got me to climax by riding me like a cowgirl and laid down next to me with what I took to be a satisfied smile on her face. I had aches in muscles I didn't even know existed and felt much better after a hot shower. Before dinner we sat on the balcony with our gin and tonics, me in my board shorts and Juliette in a cute sun dress, admiring the ocean view. The wind and surf had kicked up a bit over the course of the afternoon so there were quite a few surfers in the water.

Juliette heated up the parmas in the oven while I prepared a salad. It was the least I could do. Since it was a bit breezy, we ate inside. Roberta sure knew had to make a parma. It was better than the one I had eaten the night before.

Neither one of us had room for dessert so we sat on the recliners and watched a few minutes of the news on the ABC. Juliette was not as lively as she had been earlier. Maybe she needed a nap. I know I could have used one. She turned off the TV and we sat in silence for a few minutes.

"So, what's on the agenda for tomorrow," I asked. "Want to go some-where? I'd be happy to sit by the pool again if you are."

"There isn't going to be a tomorrow, Gary," she said.

"There isn't?"

"To be truthful Gary, the sex wasn't that good. A woman of my means can do a lot better, so I think it's best that you just go."

From the tone of her voice and the look on her face I knew she wasn't kidding.

I slowly got out of Daryl Gardner's recliner and took off the shirt she had given me to wear. Mine had gotten wet earlier and was hanging on the back of a chair in the dining area along with my baseball cap. I put the shirt on and quickly buttoned it. I took my cap and checked my pockets to make sure I had everything I arrived with.

I walked over to the recliner where Juliette was still seated, leaned over, and attempted to kiss her on the cheek. She turned away. I showed myself out and took the elevator downstairs. Halfway down I felt my ears pop. On the walk back to my motel I passed the same ice cream shop where I had stopped the night before. The line was just as long. I gave it a miss.

Swing and a Miss

Gary Delaney leaned on his golf bag and watched Ellen Jenkins grip his new TaylorMade driver and take a few practice swings.

Only one other time in her 49 years had she ever hit a golf ball and that was 25 years, three children and one soon to be ex-husband ago.

Since the local par three golf course wasn't all that busy, Ellen didn't feel that every eye was on her. If she was nervous, she didn't show it. She gently placed her Titleist on the first tee and adjusted her light blue baseball cap.

I know she can dance, but can she hit a golf ball? Delaney thought as he watched Jenkins address the ball.

Two nights earlier he looked on in amazement along with every other member of the social group he belonged to as the vivacious, charming, stunning brunette put on an exhibition of salsa and bachata dancing that left the owner of a local dance studio stunned.

"Where did you learn to dance like that?" Ellen was asked when the group took a drinks break.

"I had a lesson a few weeks ago."

"One lesson and you can dance like that?" Delaney asked on behalf of the group.

Ellen shrugged her bare shoulders as she sipped a glass of champagne.

"I don't know. When I hear that kind of music it just takes over my body."

Delaney made a mental note to himself to find out what the music was, download it and play it on a continuous loop if she ever visited his apartment.

It took the 52-year-old Delaney a few weeks to get the courage to ask Ellen out on a date. She was a bit out of his league, looks wise, but surprisingly she said yes. He suggested miniature golf and one go around the six-hole par-three course. Maybe a drink afterwards, good wholesome fun. It was mid-afternoon on a still and clear Sunday in Far North Queensland. The mosquitos had even taken the afternoon off.

Ellen planted her feet, drew back the driver, kept her head down and made solid contact with the ball. It veered off to the right a bit and landed about 110 metres away, just 10 metres or so off the green.

She looked at Delaney and had the same sort of smile on her face that a professional golfer has after birdying the 18th hole and seeing her name move to the top of the leaderboard on a late spring Sunday afternoon.

"Pretty good, huh?" she asked.

"Well, you did slice it a bit," Delaney cracked.

"Oh? Then you try wise guy," she said handing him the club.

On a good day, Delaney could break 90 over 18 holes. On a bad day he could lose half a dozen balls. He stood over his ball and took several practice swings.

Easy now, just make contact. Don't make an arse of yourself, he thought as he drew back his club.

Delaney made contact, but the driver found more grass than ball. It went about 10 feet in the air and travelled maybe 20 metres.

Ellen tried not to laugh.

"You hooked it mate," she said.

She reached into the golf bag and tossed a new ball to Delaney.

"You look a bit pale there Gary. Go on, have another go. And try to block out the fact that I also beat you at mini golf and you owe me dinner."

Flustered, it took Delaney three shots just to reach the green.

"Hand me the pitching wedge, will you mate?" Ellen asked when she reached her ball.

She lined up the shot, opened the club face and lobbed the ball five metres from the pin.

"You're away," she said handing him his putter.

Delaney's first putt missed the cup and kept on going, leaving him a seven-metre putt. He made it – barely – for a five.

"Nice shot," Ellen said. "Hand me that putter, will you please? This is for par."

She studied the hole like Jack Fucking Nicklaus and sank the putt.

"A three for me and a five for you," she said writing down the scores in pencil on the scorecard.

The second hole was a bit further, about 120 metres with a slight dog leg to the left. A bunker was just to the left of the green.

With a textbook swing off the tee, the primary school maths teacher sent her shot high into the air. The ball bounced once, hopped over the sand trap, and landed on the green.

She gave him a wink.

"Beginners luck, eh? Wait till I tell the rest of the group."

She was positively bubbling.

Delaney laughed. What else could he do?

After finishing the sixth and final hole, Jenkins and Delaney retreated to one of the several tables and chairs near the driving range which offered a bit of shade.

"Get us a couple of cold ones, will you? I'll tally up the scores," Ellen said.

He had been beaten by nearly the length of the Flemington straight – eight strokes.

"Don't take it so hard mate," Ellen said when he returned. She winked when she said it, so Delaney believed he was in with a chance. He was a gracious loser. They had a few laughs. He even got a kiss goodbye when they returned to their cars in the parking lot. However, there was no dinner, no second date.

Ellen wound up hooking up with some guy from the social group who was even better looking than she was; tall, fit and with a full head of wavy, brown hair. Together, the two looked like they had just stepped off the top of a wedding cake.

The next day Delaney rang the pro at the golf club he frequented and booked himself in for a lesson.

"How many?" he was asked.

"Keep a few dates handy. I have a feeling I am going to need them."

The College Graduate

They lined the shores of the Mississippi River in Backwater, Arkansas, by the thousands on the morning of the fourth of April in 1962 to get a glimpse of something even rarer than Big Foot.

They had heard of the creature, and some had seen photos or caught glimpses of it in a newsreel. But never had anyone in the state of Arkansas seen one in person.

At 9:14am on a calm and clear spring day, shouts rang out from several in the throng who had their binoculars trained upriver looking for the steamship which had left St Louis several days earlier.

The creature had been captured a month ago at a nightclub in Greenwich Village in lower Manhattan where he had been listening to Allen Ginsburg recite several of his best-known poems. One of the leading figures of the Beat Generation of the late 1950s and early 1960s, Ginsberg always drew a large crowd. The audience of several hundred listened intensely, nodded their heads in agreement and snapped their fingers in unison when a verse hit home.

Dressed in a beige turtleneck, dark sportscoat, black pants and loafers, David Weiss and his date, Sarah Rosenstein, were seated at a table to the side of the stage. It was a big night for Weiss, since Rosenstein, his girlfriend of four months, had promised that if he took her to see

Ginsberg, she would let him touch her breasts – through her bra – later that night when he dropped her off at home. "This is so exciting," she bubbled when Ginsberg took the stage just after 9:30pm. Weiss adjusted his wire-framed glasses, stroked his goatee, and tried to hide his hard-on.

"Far out man, far out," a middle-aged man shouted when Ginsberg started reading *Howl*, his best-known work.

Before Ginsberg took the stage, promoter Russell Adams carefully surveyed the room. Adams, a tall man who never met a meal he didn't like, was the owner of a travelling circus which featured human oddities. Recently he had received several letters and phone calls from the mayors of several towns in the deep south where his troupe had visited the previous spring and summer.

"Bring me something rare, something different," Mayor Calhoun Jackson III of Backwater, Arkansas, told Adams during a recent phone call. "We've seen enough of your bearded ladies and Siamese twins. What the folks down here want to see up close and in person is a college graduate; a live, breathing, walking, and talking college graduate. You're in New York Adams. Shit, they got more college boys there than we have hogs. Don't bother coming down this year unless you bring one. And have him bring his diploma with him. We might not be able to read it, but we want to see what one looks like."

Adams zeroed in on the crowd and spotted a fellow with a New York University jacket draped over the back of his chair. It was Weiss. He was seated close to a fire door and would be easy to bundle onto the street where a car was parked by the curb. He looked to be in his mid-20s, and with his glasses and goatee looked like a real academic which is what Jackson and the other mayors wanted.

As Ginsberg reached the conclusion of his set, Adams and two of his assistants slowly made their way to Weiss's table. It wasn't as polished an operation as Eichmann's capture in Argentina two years earlier, but it was just as effective. Before Sarah Rosenstein was able to utter a word, her boyfriend was yanked out of his chair, had a sack placed over his head, was quickly marched out the fire door, stuffed into a car and driven off.

Her cries were drowned out by applause for Ginsberg's performance. She was later told by the establishment's manager that Weiss had been arrested by the US Treasury Department for counterfeiting.

"David? A counterfeiter? No, no," she wailed.

"You don't have to worry about anything if you cooperate with us," Adams told Weiss when they arrived at his spread in rural northern New Jersey. He pulled the sack off Weiss's head when everyone was safely inside. All the curtains were drawn and since it was in the middle of the night Weiss had no idea where he was or why he had been kidnapped.

"What do you want with me?" he asked Adams, who was seated across from him. Standing on either side of Adams were his associates who dragged Weiss from the nightclub. Tank Hill and Stubby Wilson each played college football for the University of Georgia Bulldogs in the late 1950s. Both were recruited solely for their ability to stop the run and rush the quarterback. The outside linebackers rarely went to class and after playing starring roles in the Bulldogs' Cotton Bowl win over the Texas Longhorns on New Year's Day of 1960 never set foot in a classroom again. They never graduated but impregnated half of the cheerleading squad.

"I'm just a first-year associate professor at NYU for goodness sake. And where's Sarah? You haven't hurt her, have you?" Weiss asked Adams.

"She's fine," Mr Weiss. "Say, is it alright if I call you David?"

"You can call me whatever you want if you tell me what the fuck is going on?"

"Let's be civil David," Adams said as he lit a cigarette. "There's no need for that kind of language. I can assure you that Miss Rosenstein is fine."

"Care for a smoke?"

"No thank you."

"As for your question, do you ever go the circus, David?"

"The circus?"

"Yes".

"When I was a kid once or twice."

"You see David, I run a circus. And this circus of mine has oddities. Bearded ladies, midgets, conjoined twins, that sort of thing. We travel mainly through the south and my customers have heard a lot about people like you but never seen one in the flesh."

"People like me?"

Adams laughed and took a few long drags on his cigarette.

"A college graduate with an actual diploma. You see David, you are my King Kong."

"Your what?" Weiss asked.

"We are going to show the good folks of the south, a real live New York City college boy, a college graduate in the flesh."

"You can't do that with me," Weiss said raising his voice.

"Oh, I can. It will be better for you to cooperate, better for you and for Miss Rosenstein."

"You'd hurt Sarah? You're a monster."

Adams laughed. "I'm just giving the people what they want. And what they want is to see one of you. Our train leaves for St Louis in a few days. Then we'll board a ship on the Mississippi to continue our journey. Cooperate and you'll travel in the company of Tank and Stubby. If you don't, I guess we can find room with the big cats, or do you prefer reptiles for roommates?"

Tank and Stubby had Weiss covered by several hundred pounds, most of it muscle. And they smelled just as bad as they looked. Weiss was well fed through-out the trip to St Louis and again on the three-day journey down the mighty Mississippi. He was allowed to have a cigarette or two on the *Spirit of Mississippi*'s wind-swept deck. He passed when offered a sip of the bottles of some awful concoction that Tank and Stubby shared night and day.

"How the heck do they not just fall over?" Weiss asked himself. "If I drank that much I'd be in coma for a month."

He gave some thought to jumping overboard during his next cigarette break, but it was at least a 50-or-60-foot drop into the water and he wasn't the best of swimmers. "Shit. I'll wait till we're on dry land and then see if I can make a run for it."

Weiss didn't see Adams again until the ship docked in Backwater, Arkansas.

"Enjoy the trip Weiss? Stubby and Weiss are good company although the shit they drink could put a hole in anyone else's stomach."

"It was fine Mr Adams. What's next? Time for you to show me off?"

"Soon my boy, soon."

Once the ship was safely secured to the dock, Backwater, Arkansas mayor Calhoun Jackson III greeted Adams with a handshake and a bear hug.

"Just look at this crowd," the mayor said. "We haven't had a crowd this big since Elvis performed here back in the 50s. He killed 'em with *Jailhouse Rock*. Your boy doesn't sing, does he?"

"Only in the shower," Adams said, which got a big laugh from the mayor.

"You get the crowd going, give Weiss a big build-up and then we'll bring him out," Adams said.

Always the promoter, Adams had decided to put Weiss in a cage, much the way King Kong was introduced to the public when he arrived in New York in the 1933 film.

"You want me to put me in that?" Weiss said when Adams showed him the cage. "I'm not going in there. It's bad enough that you're going to show me off like some sort of freak, but I'm drawing the line. I'm not getting in it."

Adams whistled and almost instantaneously, Tank Hill and Stubby Wilson appeared. They lifted Weiss up with a couple of fingers and tossed him into the cage. Before closing it, Adams gave Weiss a diploma he purchased in St. Louis. "Hold it up nice and high when you are introduced," Adams told him.

The cage containing Weiss was covered in a green tarp and lowered by crane onto the dock.

"Easy folks," Mayor Calhoun Jackson III told the crowd which surged forward when the cage came into view. "The college boy ain't going no place, so please do not crowd the dock. Wait in line behind the barricades and have your dollar bills handy. Photos with the college boy will be a dollar extra. A family photo is $5. Exact change only."

Looking out over the crowd, Adams figured the day's takings would be close to $10,000. His contract with the mayor called for a 50-50 split. "Easiest money I'll ever make," he said as the cage was lowered onto the dock.

Adams took the microphone from the mayor and acknowledged the loud applause. "Thank you all for coming to see this rare creature. Don't get too close to the cage because college boy hasn't had his breakfast yet.

Mayor Calhoun Jackson III led the laughter, in fact he nearly pissed himself. "He hasn't had his breakfast yet," he said to the Chief of Police, Billy Joe Tallahuchi, who stood beside him. "Adams is a hoot."

Having failed to see the humour, Tallahuchi merely shrugged his shoulders.

Adams pointed to the drummer from the Backwater High School marching band, Goober Rhode, which was Rhode's cue to begin a drum roll.

"And now, without further ado, let me present to you, all the way from New York City, a genuine college graduate, Mr David Weiss."

The tarp was pulled back and the crowd's loud cheers turned to silence. Adams turned as white as a sheet. Mayor Calhoun Jackson III turned beet red. The cage was empty.

"What the fuck is going on Adams?"

I put him in the cage myself, Adams said to himself.

"I'll get him. I told ya them college boys are smarter than your average hog. Have the band play something to calm the crowd."

Adams ran back on the ship and started yelling.

"Tank? Stubby? Where the fuck are you guys? Get your asses here, now!"

Adams returned to the spot where Weiss had been loaded into the cage and found Tank and Stubby passed out next to several empty whiskey bottles snoring away.

"I told you that shit would fuck you up."

He tried rousing the two, but they didn't move.

Nor would they for at least 12 hours. The booze and the quaaludes Weiss gave them had knocked them out almost immediately.

"Weiss? Weiss?" Adams screamed.

There was no reply.

"You won't get far you son of a bitch. And when I find you, I'll feed you to the fucking lions you prick. Weiss? Weiss?"

Think Russell, think. That crowd out there will have my arse as will the mayor.

As Adams tried to figure out what to do, a lone figure, a couple of hundred yards away, jumped into one of several motorboats parked on the shoreline. "Please start," he said as he yanked the starter cord of the *Mercury* motor. The 12-footer sprung to life.

"Thank Christ," David Weiss said.

He kissed the motor.

"Now get me the fuck out of here."

The Pod

Dale Bergeron bent down like a professional golfer trying to get a read on a tricky putt, stuck his head into his sleeping quarters for the night and sighed.

Armstrong, Aldrin and Collins had more room than this when they went to the moon, he thought.

The 55-year-old newsreader and producer for a string of area radio stations was not scheduled to move into his apartment for another nine days and after having forked out close to $2800 for bond and the first month's rent was nearly tapped out.

Earlier that morning Bergeron was found sleeping on the floor of his small office by the morning disc jockey who heard snoring as he prepared for his four-hour shift.

"What the hell is going on Dale? I thought you were staying with your ex-wife until your apartment is ready to move into," Johnny Rhodes said.

"I was," Bergeron said, struggling to get up off the floor. "Give me a hand, will you? I made a few remarks about a guy she is seeing, and she asked me to leave. That was three nights ago. I've spent the last two nights at a motel and I'm all but broke so to save $100 a night ..."

He was too embarrassed to continue.

"Shit Dale. I wish I could help mate but between my wife and kids we barely have enough room for ourselves."

Bergeron had enquired about a few Airbnb properties but once he told the owners about his early to bed and early to rise hours, he was told he wouldn't be a good fit.

He was left with two options: sleep in the office or in his car. The nights were too cold to sleep in his Camry and its back seat was full of clothing and boxes of books and paperwork, so he waited until everyone left the station – the last guy to leave was Hal Sherman, the sports guy who had a 6pm to 8pm call-in show. The station ran by itself overnight; an automated system which cost three staffers their jobs more than three years ago and pumped out slick syndicated shows and ads for national chains from 8pm to 6am. Bergeron watched Hal Sherman drive off and after having turned off the building's alarm walked straight past the reception desk into the kitchen/lounge area and flicked on the TV.

The only lights he turned on were the florescent ones in the kitchen/lounge and the one in his small office. He made himself a coffee and after a couple of hours of switching back and forth between an overseas cricket match and CNN, turned the TV off, washed up in the men's toilet and tried to get some sleep in his office. His desk chair and a hi-back chair in the corner by the door were much too uncomfortable to sleep in so he rolled up a towel to use as a pillow, draped his coat around him and went to sleep on the floor. He intended to set his phone alarm for 5:15 but somehow forgot which led to him being discovered fast asleep by Johnny Rhodes, who was also the station manager.

"I'm sorry Dale, but you can't sleep here again. There are insurance regulations the station would be in violation of."

Rhodes, whose real name was Henry Kominski, peeled off four $50 notes from his billfold and tried to give them to Bergeron, who pushed his hand away.

"It's not a gift mate. Pay me back when we get paid next week, or even the two weeks after that."

Bergeron reluctantly took the money and stuffed the notes into his front pocket. "Thanks Hank. I appreciate it."

"Don't mention it. We're on the air in just 25 minutes so we better get a wriggle on."

"Anything of note happen overnight?"

"At a black-tie gathering in Perth honouring the mining company which shipped the most iron ore to China over the past 12 months, Julie Bishop tripped in her trademark red high heels and took a tumble. Gina Reinhart was standing next to her and cradled her like an appetizer. There's great video of it which you can bet all the morning shows will lead with. There's day 100 of the latest government shutdown in the US. Oh, and some sex scandal in Hollywood with that director Dick Foreskin, or whatever the hell his name is, the guy with the neck tattoo."

Bergeron laughed for the first time in days.

"It will make for one entertaining news bulletin," he said.

After a quick trip to the toilet, a brief look at his Twitter feed and a few minutes putting his bulletin together, Bergeron's smooth voice boomed out over the airwaves on the stroke of 6am. "Good morning, Tasmania. It's 6am. I'm Dale Bergeron and here's what's making news this morning ..."

The guy is a pro. A few hours of sleep on a floor, nothing but lint in his pockets and he sounds like Walter "Fucking" Cronkite, Johnny Rhodes thought as Bergeron's voice filled his headphones.

The news of Collingwood champion Sam Brass's fling with exotic dancer Ophelia Knobb two weeks before the start of finals topped the sports news. The weather followed – temps in the low teens for much of the state with more clouds than sun. A jingle and a procession of trumpets announced Rhodes's arrival. Twenty-five minutes later Bergeron did it all over again. He kept the reports of Bishop and Brass in, took a handful of other items out and replaced them with fresh news. There was occasionally a bit of banter between Rhodes and Bergeron at the top of each hour, with Rhodes playing the part of the out-of-control DJ and Bergeron the voice of reason. After the 10am bulletin, the entertaining Joey Rodgers took over the airwaves. He hammered local politicians, got listeners fired up for causes close to his heart and was exhausted by the time his three-hour shift was over. Most days his voice became hoarse, and his shirt was stained by sweat as the studio clock ticked towards 1pm. In the last ratings period both Rhodes and Rodgers were pulling 20 shares. They were so popular, would-be advertisers were forced to go on a waiting list.

Bergeron's last newscast of the day was at 12 noon. He usually hung around the station until 2pm, working on bits he and Rhodes would do the following day. As he had done the past few days Bergeron stayed back to have a look at the Airbnb and Gumtree websites on his office computer. He was looking for a place to stay for the next nine days.

His bed, TV, fridge, couch, desk, dining room table, washing machine and other odds and ends were in storage patiently waiting to be moved into his new apartment. The flat was close to 20 years old but in excellent nick after having been renovated only a year earlier. Bergeron just had to wait for its present tenants to vacate and clean the property before he could move in on the first of the month.

He couldn't find anything new on Airbnb or Gumtree, but he did notice an advert for a hotel called The Pod. It wasn't a hotel in the traditional sense of the word although it did provide a bed, linen, towels and even breakfast in a common area decked out with several large tables and chairs. It was $50 a night and not even five minutes from the station. He called to see if there were any vacancies, – there were – and decided to go over and have a look.

An Asian fellow at the reception desk looked up from his meal and greeted Bergeron. "You're the fellow I spoke to on the phone? Yes?"

"I am. Can you give me the grand tour?"

The third year University of Tasmania student showed him the common areas and the bathrooms first and then led him to the sleep pods.

"Where'd you get these? From the sets of *Lost in Space* and *Star Trek*?" Bergeron asked.

"No, no," Billy Cheng said. "These are brand new, beds barely slept in."

There were six pods at ground level and another six stacked on top of them bunk-bed style. There were 12 more on the other side of the room and another 48 scattered throughout other parts of the complex. Each pod had its own entrance. The pods opened with the swipe of a card. *It's a good thing I'm not claustrophobic*, he said to himself.

"Can I try it out?" he asked.

"Sure."

Bergeron sat on the double bed and laid down on his back. The ceiling was not even four feet above him. *It's like being in a fucking coffin*, he thought.

"These are soundproof?"

"Yes. Once you close the pod's door you won't hear a thing."

The mattress was comfortable enough as was the pillow, so he decided to try it for a night.

Back at reception Bergeron filled out the necessary paperwork and handed over one of the four $50 notes Kominski had given him.

Just after 2am Bergeron was coming back from the bathrooms after trying to squeeze out his third piss of the night when he nearly collided with a young woman trying to locate her pod.

"Can you help me find number 16?" she asked.

"I'm in number eight so I'm guessing your pod is across from mine," Bergeron said pointing to another stack of the space-age contraptions.

I know that voice, the woman thought. Lights at either end of the hallway were bright enough for her to confirm that it was indeed Dale Bergeron.

"Dale? What are you doing here?"

Shit, Bergeron said to himself.

"Is that you Darcy?"

Darcy Hall was one of the young reporters from the station. She was barely 25 years old and everyone knew of her desire to work in television. Her videotapes, along with thousands of others, were stacked in the offices of every network in Australia. Bergeron was sure she would wind up in Sydney or Melbourne one day and it was not just because of her looks; from his years of experience, he knew she was one hell of a reporter.

"It is. What are you doing here?" she asked again.

"You first."

"I'm doing a story on these pod hotels. They're catching on everywhere."

Makes sense, he thought.

"Why am I here? I'll tell you but can you please keep this between you and me? It's downright embarrassing."

"I won't say a word."

"I'm in between apartments. I can't move into my new one until the current tenants leave – which is in nine more days – and I can't afford to stay at a hotel. Fifty bucks a night is about all I can spend."

"Geez."

"I know, sad, eh? I hope you didn't get into radio for the money Darcy. Look at me. After 25 years in the business, I'm sleeping in a freaking pod."

He sounds just like my dad did when he and Mum got divorced, Darcy thought. *Defeated. But what can I do?*

"Don't worry Dale. It's just temporary. And it really isn't so bad here. The beds are comfortable, the place is clean. Coffee and toast are free."

"Thanks Darcy. But remember, this is just between us."

Darcy nodded.

"Look, it's been nice chatting, but I've got to get back into my pod. I need to get up in a couple of hours."

"Okay. Goodnight Dale. And Dale ..."

"Yes?"

"Take your protein pill and put your helmet on."

Bergeron was woken at 4:45 by the alarm on his phone. He put his pyjamas on the double bed, stuck his size 11 feet into an old pair of slippers and fastened a towel around his waist. He grabbed his bag of toiletries, tossed his phone on the bed, closed, and locked his pod, and walked to the bathroom.

As far as he could tell he was the only one up. He showered, brushed his teeth and on the way back to his pod removed a small overnight bag from the locker he was given. He quickly dressed, put all his belongings back in the locker and made his way to the common area. The only person he saw was an older guy manning the front desk.

"You're up early mate," he said to Bergeron.

"Yup, I've got a paper run. Put me down for another two nights please. Pod number eight. The name's Bergeron."

He handed the fellow $100 and was given a receipt. Bergeron had just $50 left from the $200 Kominski had given him plus another $100 or so in cash. He had less than $20 in his bank account. His lone credit card was maxed out.

Bergeron made himself a cup of coffee and popped two pieces of bread into the toaster. He checked the ABC's website on his phone to see if anything major had happened while he slept, washed his dishes after he was done eating and looked at his watch. It was 5:25. *I better be on my way*, he said to himself.

As he drove to the station on the dark, empty roads, Bergeron sized up his situation. He had eight more nights to get through before he could move into his apartment. The next two nights were paid for. He didn't have a clue where he would spend the other six.

His daydreaming came to a sudden halt when a dog came out of nowhere and ran right in front of his car. Bergeron slammed on the brakes and felt the seatbelt dig into his stomach and shoulder. He put the car in park and jumped out to see if he had hit it. He hadn't, but it was a very close call. Another foot and the young golden retriever would have taken its last poop. Bergeron bent down to comfort the frightened animal. It had a collar and a licence but would not move. Bergeron lifted her off the cold pavement and placed her in the front seat.

"It's alright girl. We'll get you back to your home as soon as we can," he said, stroking the dog's soft coat. "But you'll have to come to the station with me, okay? I'm on the air in 30 minutes."

He carried the dog inside and placed it in his office. "I'll be right back," he said. In the kitchen he filled up a bowl of water and brought it to his office. Bergeron watched the dog lap it up. *She can't be more than four months old*, he thought.

"The council doesn't open until 8:30 so you're going to have to stay here for a few hours, okay?" he said. The dog didn't hear a word. It had fallen asleep.

"Where'd you spend the night, Dale? Find anyplace?" Kominski asked Bergeron as he walked into the studio a few minutes before the 6am newscast.

"In a pod."

"In a what?"

"A pod. Fifty bucks a night. I'll tell you about it when we break for commercials."

Before Bergeron read the sports and weather, he announced that a lost dog had been found, was safe at the station and urged the owner to ring the contest line. He gave out the number every half hour. Two hours later there hadn't been one call.

A couple of kilometres away single mother Susan Douglas asked her youngest daughter Hailey to feed their dog of three months before she fixed her own breakfast.

"You and your sister promised you'd look after the dog, remember?"

"Yes Mum," the eight-year-old answered.

Hailey picked Goldie's food bowl off the kitchen floor, filled it with a combination of dry and canned puppy food and called the pooch's name.

"Goldie, your tucker is ready. Goldie."

Usually, Goldie ran into the kitchen as soon as she heard her name. Her bed in the living room was just a few steps away from a doggie door the family had recently installed. Goldie came and went as she pleased during the night, sparing Hailey and her sister Laurie, and their mum of getting up every couple of hours to let the dog in and out.

Despite Hailey's repeated shouts, Goldie failed to materialise.

"Check the backyard," Susan Douglas told her daughter. "Maybe she is out having a wee."

Hailey called Goldie's name and walked around the good-sized yard but couldn't find her. She wasn't in her kennel either. Hailey went back in the house.

"Mum. Goldie's not in the yard. Did she run away?" Hailey asked.

"Laurie, go have a look will you sweetheart? Mummy's running a little late this morning."

Susan Douglas had an important staff meeting at 9:15 and was being extra careful with her hair and make-up. The 39-year-old had recently passed her realtor's exam and was hoping to be promoted from receptionist to full-time real estate agent at Petrie Realty. There was a vacancy after the sudden departure of realtor Nancy Sinclair, and agency boss Mathias Petrie preferred to promote from within.

A few minutes later Hailey and Laurie came back inside. "She's gone Mum. There's a piece of the fence missing," Laurie reported.

Tears started to run down Hailey's face. "Is she coming back Mum? Is she?"

"Of course, she is sweetheart," Susan told her daughter as she held her.

"Laurie, show me where Goldie got out."

Laurie led the way to the broken fence.

Susan picked up a plank which was in the neighbour's yard and examined another which had been pushed out of place. *I knew the dog was strong, but how the heck was she able to get out?* she thought.

"Let's go to the Bennett's. Maybe they've got Goldie," Susan told her daughters.

Susan knocked on the front door which Jan Bennett opened almost immediately.

"Sorry to bother you so early Jan. Our puppy Goldie has gotten out of the backyard. Have you or Jim seen her?" she asked the retiree, who was in her nightgown.

Jan Bennett motioned for Susan and her two daughters to come into her kitchen. The sound of a newscast from a radio on the countertop filled the room. "Can I get you a cuppa Susan?"

"Thanks, but no. We're running a little late. Did you see our dog?"

"I haven't Susan. I'm sorry. Jim had an early tee time. He would have told me if he had seen her. What's her name again?"

"Goldie, Goldie," Hailey screamed out as tears again filled her eyes. Susan put her arms around her daughter to comfort her when she heard Dale Bergeron announce that a lost dog had been found and was at the station. "Everyone, hush," she yelled.

"The dog is a golden retriever or labrador about four or five months old and is safe here at the station. She has a blue collar and is registered. If this is your dog or you know whose it might be, please ring the station's contest line: 6428 4444. That number again, 6428 4444. If we don't hear from anyone by 9am we'll get in touch with the local council, and it will attempt to locate the dog's owner.

"What was the number?" Susan screamed. "Did anyone get that number?"

"6428 4444," Laurie Douglas said.

Since Susan had run out the door without her phone, she asked Jan if she could use hers.

"Of course, dear. "It's right here on the wall."

Susan punched in the number and waited for someone to pick up.

"Newsroom," a familiar voice said.

"I think you have our dog," Susan told Dale Bergeron. "How is she?"

"The dog is fine. She's sleeping in my office."

While the two talked Goldie was taking a wee and a large poop on the worn rug in Bergeron's small office.

"What's the dog's name Miss?"

"Goldie."

"Hold the line. Let me see if she answers to it."

Bergeron opened the door to his office and took a few backward steps as a putrid smell filled his nostrils. "Fuck me," he said softly.

"Goldie," he called. The moment the dog heard her name, her ears perked up. She ran to Bergeron and nearly knocked him over. "I think we can safely assume you're Goldie," he told the dog as he tried to settle it. Bergeron took a necktie off the chair in the corner, tied it around the dog's collar and walked back to the phone as Goldie nipped at his heels.

"I'm pretty sure this is your dog," he told Susan Douglas. "When can you come by the station and pick her up?"

"I'll be there in five minutes."

"You know where we are?"

"Sure do. I drive past the station every day."

"Let's go girls. Goldie is at the radio station."

Susan Douglas thanked Jan Bennett and ran back to her house to grab her phone and keys. Four minutes later she knocked on the front door of the station. Knowing who was on the other side, Goldie was jumping at the door as Bergeron opened it.

"Thank you so much," Susan said as she attached a lead to Goldie's collar.

"Where did you find her?"

"On the main road. About 5:30 it was."

Bergeron left out the details about coming within a few inches of hitting her. "I pulled over, picked her up, put her in the car and brought her to the station. Do you know how she got out?"

"She knocked over part of the backyard fence."

"I can believe that. She is one strong dog."

"And she's getting bigger and stronger every day. Kids, put Goldie in the car please."

Susan Douglas and Dale Bergeron each checked their watches at the same time.

"I've got to run, get the kids to school, fix a fence and then go to work. Thank you so much ..."

"Dale. Dale Bergeron."

"The newsman?"

"That's me. You'll have to excuse me. I've got a bulletin in 10 minutes and an office to clean up."

"She didn't, did she?"

"She did. But it's not too bad. I'll call in the hazardous materials team, open a window and within a few weeks it will as good as new."

Susan Douglas laughed, thanked Bergeron again, got in her car and sped off. She had 40 minutes to drop the girls off at school, hammer the missing fence planks back into place, finish getting dressed and get to work. "What a morning," she said when she finally took her seat at the reception desk at 9:02.

After finishing the 8:30 bulletin, Bergeron grabbed a fistful of paper towels and a couple of bottles of cleaning products from the kitchen and went to his office. He nearly gagged from the stench, opened the office's lone window, scooped up the poop with a piece of cardboard and chucked it into a plastic bag. He carried it outside and dumped it into a trash can out back. On his way back inside, he grabbed the can of air freshener from the men's toilet and gave his office a good spray. "It's no use," he said later that morning, "I'm going to have to get the carpet steam cleaned. But with what? I don't have a pot to piss in."

Bergeron spent the next two nights at The Pod and the next six at an Airbnb costing $70 a night after persuading an older couple to take a $100 deposit and then the $320 balance in two weeks when he got his next paycheque.

On his first night at the Airbnb, a Sunday, he climbed into bed around 8:30 and set his phone alarm for 4:15am. Bergeron put his head on a comfortable pillow and drifted off to sleep only to be awakened soon after by the sound of a dog barking.

"You've got to be kidding," he said. He got out of bed and looked out the window of the two-storey house. It overlooked the backyard of the house next door. The barking dog was illuminated by an outdoor light likely set off by a motion detector. He opened the window, looked at the dog and did a double take.

"Goldie? Is that you?"

Goldie looked up. "Stay right there," Bergeron said in a firm voice. "I have a carpet cleaning bill with your name on it."

The Package

"**O**rdinarily I wouldn't ask, but I need a favour," read the text message.

The sender was a mate of mine, and I began to wonder what the favour was. *Finals footy tickets? A loan? Borrow my car?*

Wrong, wrong, and wrong.

Bryan Miller, or "DC" as he was known due to his fondness for Diet Coke, wanted me to deliver a package for him – to a retirement home in Launceston.

"Couldn't you just post it?" I texted back. "It would get there by tomorrow."

His reply came 30 seconds later. "He may not last until tomorrow. He's very ill mate, very ill and I'm swamped at work and can't get away."

Since I had the rest of the morning and afternoon free, as I do every day – one of the pluses of retirement – I agreed.

"Meet me at my office if you could around 11:30. I'll put the package in your hands along with directions. It's a little tricky to find."

I pulled my SUV into his office parking lot on Oldaker St at 11:25. DC was waiting outside, pacing like an expectant father, an unlit cigarette in his hands.

"I'm trying to quit," the 55-year-old accountant said.

The package was not large, smaller than a shoebox. The name Joe Cameron was printed on a label with the street name and suburb.

DC said it contained a letter and some personal items that he wanted his former mentor to have a look at before he passed away. "Bring it to reception and tell them it is for Mr Cameron."

I carefully laid the package on the passenger seat of my Honda and told DC I'd take care of it. He thanked me profusely and went back inside the two-storey building where a Diet Coke was waiting on his desk along with the Andretti File.

I punched the street name and suburb into the Google Maps app on my phone and took off for Kings Meadows. Shady Acres Rest Home was exactly 100km away. Despite a steady rain which started near the turn-off to Deloraine, I made good time and arrived in Launceston an hour and 10 minutes later. The sweet, friendly voice of the Google Maps lady seamlessly guided me into Kings Meadows. Two left turns later, however, she abruptly changed direction.

"At the next roundabout, unbutton your shirt," she ordered.

I checked the phone to see what was going on. Everything seemed to be in order.

"In 200 metres take a right and remove your pants," the woman continued.

"Excuse me? I replied. Nevertheless, I did as she said. But my left pants leg got caught on my shoe which nearly caused me to crash through a white-picket fence and into someone's front yard.

When the car came to a stop on the nature strip, I wiped the sweat from my brow and remembered why I was in Launceston. I hitched my pants back up, buttoned my shirt and un-plugged the app. I decided to find Shady Acres the old-fashioned way – I pulled into a nearby service station and got directions.

I was less than two kilometres away. Five minutes later I pulled into the grounds of Shady Acres. The lawns were a lush green, and several flower beds were bursting with colour. The parking lot was half empty even though it was visiting hour.

I took the package and locked the car just in case a resident was looking for an after-lunch joy ride. Above the doors on the brick building 15 metres in front of me was a sign reading reception. The electric doors peeled back as I approached, giving me the feeling that I had stepped onto the flight deck of the USS *Enterprise*.

I walked to the front desk where one woman was tapping away at her computer. Another had her head buried in a stack of folders on her desk. The dinner menu was printed on a chalk board to my left. Green salad, pumpkin soup, fish (grilled) with chips and veggies. Sticky date pudding was for dessert along with tea and coffee.

"Excuse me," I said. Both women looked up. The one on the computer came to the front desk.

"I have a package here for Mr Joe Cameron. Would you be able to see that he gets this right away?"

"You can give it to him yourself if you like." She pointed to a large room to her right. "That's him, in the blue pants and white shirt leading the line dancing."

"The line dancing?"

"Yes. Every Wednesday afternoon."

I took a few steps to my left and looked in. A spritely, dapperly dressed man with white shoes, who at first glance appeared to be about 80, was giving instruction to a group of about 20 men and women. Four of them needed the use of their walkers. A Garth Brooks song was blasting from an old CD player. I waited until it ended and approached Mr Cameron.

"Mr Cameron. I'm a friend of Bryan Miller. He asked me to deliver this package to you right away."

I handed it to him and looked him over. He was fit enough to play in a Masters game of footy.

"You look a little surprised mate. Anything wrong?"

"Well, I was told by Bryan that you were on your last leg. I expected to find you in a bed with an oxygen mask on your face surrounded by family with a priest giving you last rites."

A large laugh bellowed from his six-foot frame.

"Bryan always did have a great sense of humour. How far have you driven?"

"From Devonport, 100ks each way."

He laughed again and opened the package.

"Be right with you folks," he said to the group of line dancers.

"Mind if I ask what's in the package?"

"I do. It's personal mate."

"Understood."

Cameron placed the package next to the CD player and tossed in a new disc. The opening bars of a Dwight Yoakam song, one which I knew, *A Thousand Miles from Nowhere*, got the rest of the old-timers off their seats and back on their feet.

Cameron waved to me as he taught the group the steps.

Geez, he's damn good.

I waited until the song finished and walked out of the building.

I had an hour plus drive back home to plot a return prank on Bryan but couldn't think of a decent one.

Bored with the radio I looked at my phone. *What the hell*, I said to myself. I turned the Google Maps app back on.

"With your left hand, reach up and undo my bra," the sweet voice said. "Then ..."

Shells

Vinny Pistachio took off his reading glasses, laid them on the kitchen table and rubbed his blood-shot eyes.

"It can't be," he said to himself. He picked the simple pair of spectacles up, not one of those trendy, overpriced huge, black-framed jobs that anyone south of the age of 40 is hiding half of their face with, put them on his nose and again looked at the racing pages of his morning paper. Thursday's results the bright red headline read. And underneath were the results from Kilmore, which had a card during the day and from Pakenham, which staged eight races under lights. Sixteen sets of horses's names, jockeys, trainers, winning times, and margins of victory along with the win, place, exacta, quinella, trifecta, duet, first four and quaddie pay-offs, both early and late, were all there.

Pistachio, who went by the nickname "Shells" since his study, car and desk at work were covered in red pistachio shells – you wouldn't expect a guy named Pistachio to eat avocados, would you? – checked the date of the paper at the top of the page. Thursday, May 16, 2018.

The 45-year-old took his cup of coffee with him as he rose from his chair and walked over to a calendar – a freebee he got from his local pharmacy – which hung on the wall of his study. Under a photo of a disgusting ingrown, overgrown, and brownish toenail and an accompanying ad for a miracle fungal cream, Shells ran his finger over the dates beneath it. Monday, May 13, Tuesday, May 14, Wednesday May 15, Thursday, May 16.

Shells lifted his mobile phone out of the pocket of his blue robe and checked the date; Thursday, May 16. He went back into the kitchen and looked at the racing pages once again, Thursday's results. But TODAY is Thursday. It was just after 8am. The first of eight races at Kilmore would not be run for another four and a half hours. He stroked his chin. "This has to be some sort of joke," he said to himself. "But who would go to the time, effort and money of putting a fake page in my newspaper? Simon? Nah. Dave? Not a chance. They have their hands full with their young kids, their wives and their high-falutin jobs."

Shells punched racing.com into his phone and looked at the day's entries on the website.

First race; a maiden over 1450 metres, a field of 10 with four emergencies. The early morning favourite was the number one horse: Sinking Ship. It was to be ridden by apprentice Tommy Walker. The four-year-old gelding was trained by Brian Leary, whose operation was based out of Flemington.

Shells looked at his newspaper's racing page. Sure enough, under the results, Sinking Ship was listed as the winner, paying $2.80 with Type Setter second and Redundancy third. The place prices were $1.40, $4.60 and $2.10. The exacta paid $38.60 and the trifecta $206. The first four with Smashed Avocado paid $662.

"What the heck is going on here? The results before the races are run? Am I dreaming?"

He strode into his bedroom where his wife Sarah was doing her yoga exercises.

"Sarah. You have got to see this," he yelled, thrusting the paper in her direction.

"Not now, I'm busy."

"But Sarah. You won't believe this."

"Later," Sarah said, as she stretched out on her blue yoga mat.

Shells stuck the paper right in front of Sarah's face. "Look at this, will ya?"

"Alright. But then leave me alone for 10 minutes so I can finish."

"I will. I will."

"What am I supposed to be looking at?"

"What day is today," Shells asked his wife of 12 years.

"It's Thursday, the day that follows Wednesday and precedes Friday."

Shells rolled his eyes. "Now look at this, what does it say?" Shells asked pointing to the heading.

"Thursday results."

"And what day is today?"

"Thursday."

"Don't you see what's going on here?"

"No."

"These are the results for today's races, races which haven't been run yet."

"They are not."

"Oh yes they are. I checked."

He took a $10 bill off his bedside table and ran out the front door – in his robe and slippers – birthday presents from Sarah two months earlier – onto Citation Lane. His neighbour's paper was still there, wrapped in plastic. After a few frustrating attempts he peeled the plastic off and opened it to the racing pages. The results of all eight races run the previous afternoon at Sandown were there while entries for Kilmore and Pakenham were on the opposite page.

"This can't be," he mumbled to himself as he walked to the newsagent two blocks away.

"Mummy, why is that man in his bathrobe," an eight-year-old girl asked her mum as they passed him in their SUV.

"I don't know sweetheart," she told her. *Maybe his wife just tossed him out*, she thought to herself. *If only I could get the courage to do that to your lying, cheating prick of a father.*

Oblivious to the glances of those rushing to the train station and the hundreds of kids making their way to school, Shells walked into the newsagent and strode straight to the stacks of newspapers. He picked up a copy of the paper he received at home and checked the racing pages. Thursday's entries for Kilmore and Pakenham, and Wednesday's results for Sandown.

He looked at the other daily paper – the right-wing tabloid which he never bought – and turned to its racing pages.

It too had Thursday's entries for Kilmore and Pakenham and Wednesday's results for Sandown.

He then pulled papers from the middle of the two stacks, being careful not to make a mess of things, and looked at them too: Thursday's entries for Kilmore and Pakenham and Wednesday's results for Sandown.

Shells took a copy of the paper he had at home to the register, gave the young girl the tenner he had with him and flew out the front door before realising he had forgotten his change.

"I knew I forgot something," he said on his return to the counter. He jammed the change into his robe pocket and quickly walked out the front door.

"You forgot your pants, shoes and shirt," the girl behind the register said.

Shells never heard her. He was already halfway home.

Just about out of breath, Shells compared the paper to the one he had on his dining room table.

"You went out dressed like that?" Sarah asked as she poured herself a cup of coffee. "What's wrong with you?"

"Hold on a sec."

Shells compared every page of the two papers. It didn't take very long since he had just 40 pages to flip through. Every page seemed to be identical except for the racing page.

"It can't be. This is either the biggest practical joke of all time or a gift from God to make up for my years of suffering," he said.

"What suffering? You've suffered?" Sarah asked.

"Are you new here? You have met my mother, haven't you?"

"Fair point."

Sarah looked down at the papers splashed across their dining room table.

"Now, in plain English, can you tell me just what is going on here?"

"It's like I said before. The paper that was delivered to the house today has the results of today's races before they have been run. I checked the neighbour's paper, the one who nobody knows anything about, the same one who sleeps until noon, and it is like the one I just brought back from the newsagent. Our paper is the only one – so far – which is different.

And it could be the only one out there."

"So, what are you going to do? Blow off work and go to the TAB or to the track?"

Shells put his arms on Sarah's shoulders and looked straight into her blue eyes.

"Honey, if I have today's winners here, I'll be able to blow off work at the age of 45 – for good."

Pistachio was in his third year as town planner at his local council and already was tired of being overruled time and time again by councillors and VCAT, and seeing builders, most of them millionaires many times over, turning formerly quaint suburbs into giant parking lots over his objections.

"So, you are not going in?"

"I will. Just for a couple of hours. I have a 10am meeting with a residential group that I can't miss. Some bloke wants to build a bunch of townhouses on a quiet street in Elmsford and the residents are outraged. I'm with them on this," Pistachio said. "I may be the only one. I reckon that builder has gotten his hands into the pockets of several of our councillors."

"That doesn't surprise me," Sarah said. "But seriously, you don't actually think you have the winners of today's races in your hands, do you?"

"We'll find out about 12:32 once the first race is run and won."

"Until then, what do you say we concentrate on our jobs. You have about 20 minutes to get dressed."

"Okay hun." Pistachio kissed his wife on the cheek and took the page of his paper with him into the bedroom. Twenty minutes later he was in his jacket and tie and ready to go. The newspaper page was safely tucked into his jacket pocket. But just to be in the safe side he took a picture of the Kilmore and Pakenham results with his phone. *Always pays to have a copy*, he said to himself.

Sarah Morgan had refused to take the name of Pistachio when the pair were married in a quiet ceremony a dozen years earlier and Shells couldn't blame her. They hadn't had any kids, not for a lack of trying, which was one less thing they might have argued about.

"My son is not going to be called Peter Pistachio."

"But that was my father's name."

"I don't care if his name was Charlie Cashew. The last names of our children will be Morgan, not Pistachio, and that's final."

Shells never brought it up again.

Sarah and Vinny had their first meal together a dozen years ago at a cafe a short walk from the same council office where they each still worked. She was answering the council's phones at the time while Pistachio was assistant town planner. They worked on different floors and exchanged hellos and some small talk when they found themselves in the same elevator. He was a head taller than her and after their first meeting she started wearing shoes with a decent-sized heel just in case there were any future encounters. Sarah was 5-foot-4 and usually dated men no taller than 5-foot-10 so she would not have to constantly look up at them.

Pistachio was nearly 6-foot-2. The heels killed Sarah's feet, so she started to keep a pair of flats at her desk which she wore all day until quitting time. It was the opposite of what many of her friends did, sneakers for travel, heels for the office.

Pistachio had a fondness for chicken schnitzel sandwiches and after a few failed attempts found a cafe that made a good one, a real good one at a very fair price. The schnitzels were baked, not deep fried and the cafe was close to the office so that is where he went every day. He preferred to eat away from the office unlike many who sat glued to their computer screens from 9 to 5. If there was anything urgent, he always had his phone on him.

The cafe had jugs of water at each table so there was no need to buy a can of sugar to wash down the sandwich and it also had plenty of copies of the Melbourne tabloid scattered about which he glanced at while he ate.

One Thursday afternoon around 1:15, Pistachio was seated at a table with his back to the door, scarfing down his sandwich, always on rye bread with lettuce and a bit of mayo, when Sarah Morgan came in, her feet aching in her three-inch heels.

She usually brought her lunch with her to save herself seven or eight dollars a day but being that it was a sunny spring day, she decided to go out. She was waiting in line to place her order when she noticed Pistachio sitting at the only table with a spare chair. She quickly grabbed the small mirror she carried in her purse, tousled her hair, checked her make-up and without knowing ordered the exact same sandwich that Pistachio was halfway through.

She grabbed a diet coke from the large cooler, which was stocked with every known soft and energy drink on the market, paid a young Asian fellow at the counter and then was told to take a seat. "We'll bring it over to you," he said.

Sarah took a deep breath and approached Pistachio's table. "Is this seat taken?" she asked. Pistachio looked up from the sports pages of the paper and wiped his mouth. "Not at all, plenty of room." he said rising from his chair.

"I haven't seen you for a while Sarah. Any troublemakers call in this morning?

"No. But there is always this afternoon."

"Sure is. I for one will be glad to see the end of this day."

"Problems upstairs?"

"Any time councillors and developers get together there are always problems. But it usually sorts itself out."

Just then Sarah's sandwich was brought to the table. "Here you go, enjoy it," said the same fellow who was manning the register.

"I will." Sarah spread a napkin over her lap and opened her can of Diet Coke. She picked up half of her sandwich and took a bite.

"Looks like we ordered the same lunch," Pistachio said.

"Have we?"

"Schnitzel on rye with lettuce and mayo. I have it every day. Who do you think is keeping this place in business?"

"You have the same thing every day?"

"Yup," Pistachio said, finishing off the last of his sandwich.

"I must admit it's pretty good, but don't you get tired of it?"

"Nah. When I find a winner, I tend to stick with it."

Sarah suddenly felt a bit self-conscious since she was the only one eating. She still had half a sandwich to get through.

Every time Pistachio spoke Sarah took a bite from her sandwich. She ate faster than she usually did just to finish the darn thing off and washed it all down with what was left of her soda.

Sarah went on a bit of a fishing expedition with her next question.

"Do you have anyone at home to cook for you?"

"No. I live alone. How about you?"

"Up until a few months ago I had a roommate, but she moved out to go live with her boyfriend. So, it is just me now."

"I see. Looking for another one to help with the rent?"

"No. I think I'm past the age of having a roommate. I turned 30 this year."

"You're 30?" Pistachio asked. "I would have guessed 25."

Sarah smiled. "Thank you. And you?"

"How old do you think I am?"

Sarah looked him over, not a single grey strand amid a full head of dark hair, teeth still white, no glasses. "I'll say 29."

"Close. I'm a member of the 30 club as well. Turned 30 two months ago."

"How long do you get for lunch? I don't want to get you in trouble," he asked.

"Forty-five minutes and would you believe that supervisor of mine keeps tabs on us too."

Sarah looked at her watch and picked up her handbag. "I better get going. It was nice having lunch with you."

"Mind if I walk back with you?"

"Not at all."

Pistachio took his jacket off his chair, put it on and gave the fellows behind the counter a wave as he made his way to the door.

The two parted ways when the elevator in the council building stopped on the second floor.

But just as Pistachio was about to ask Sarah what she was doing for dinner later, the elevator door closed right in his face. He pressed the button to reopen the door, but it was too late. The elevator was on the move – to the sixth floor and the offices of the planning department.

Sarah took off her heels when she got back to her desk, rubbed her aching feet, replaced them with her flats and put her headset on.

"She is going to think I am such a jerk," Pistachio said to himself as he arrived on the sixth floor. She basically asked me to have lunch with her."

Don't we have a list of all council employees somewhere? he wondered.

He went to the council homepage and went through the various departments until he found reception and Sarah Morgan's office number and email address.

He wrote an email.

And that's how it started. A few lunches led to dinner; a few dinners developed into staying the night – always at her place – something about having the home-court advantage. A few months later they found a place closer to work and moved in together which saved Sarah a small fortune every month. "He makes me laugh and is so good to me," she told her best friend Janet Reilly over drinks after work one Friday night. "And I'm able to put some money away each week. But those bloody pistachio shells of his turn up everywhere, even in our bed."

"I'd be happy to take him off your hands," Janet said. "He's kind of cute and I wouldn't mind having some nuts in my bed for a change."

Sarah Morgan worked her way up the council ladder and became the assistant to the chief executive. Pistachio took on the role of town planner after his superior was caught having one too many free dinners with several large developers who had designs on one of the local golf courses.

They moved into a nicer place, went on holidays over Christmas and every August to escape the cold Melbourne winter and dined with friends and each other's families a couple of times a month.

When Pistachio's 10am meeting broke up an hour later, he told his administrative assistant he would be out of the office for the rest of the day. Pistachio stuck his hand inside his jacket pocket. The day's racing page was safely there.

"Personal reasons," he said to Jacquie Carroll. "If it's something that can't wait, ring my mobile."

Pistachio stopped at a local TAB and plunked down $100 on Sinking Ship at the fixed odds price of $3.20 to win the first race at Kilmore.

"I've got to see this play out in person," he said.

The drive to Kilmore, 60 kilometres north of the city, took nearly 75 minutes. Pistachio arrived at the track just as the horses for the opener left the mounting yard.

He had a good look at Sinking Ship as it trotted to the starting gate on the backstretch for the 1450m race. Being a workday there wasn't much of a crowd trackside on the sunny 16° May afternoon. Strappers, trainers, and owners outnumbered Pistachio and his fellow punters. The lone on-course bookmaker was having a very quiet start to his afternoon. Not one person drifted his way to have a look at his odds.

As the field milled around the starting gate, Sinking Ship tightened into $2.90 on the tote and went off the $2.80 favourite. So far, Pistachio's newspaper – fake or not – was spot on.

When the gates crashed back Sinking Ship took a sit right behind the leaders who were going along at a decent clip. Walker angled Sinking Ship to the outside as the horses straightened for the run home. He caught the leader at the 150m mark and safely held off the fast-closing Type Setter, which placed second. Redundancy battled away to place third.

The numbers 4, 10 and 6 went up on the infield tote board. Pistachio took the racing page from his jacket pocket and looked at the results of the first from Kilmore; 4, 10 and 6.

"Holy crap," Pistachio said. The prices announced by track announcer Adam Anderson were the same as those on the racing page. He kissed the page. "I can't believe it. This is real, this is real."

He tucked the page back into his pocket and rang Sarah.

"The paper was right, the paper was right," he barked.

"Who is this?" Sarah jokingly asked.

"I had a $100 on the first race and the horse won. Not only that, but the other placegetters also matched what was in the paper."

"You're kidding me," aren't you?"

"I'm not Sarah. I'm going to walk out of here with a fortune."

"Are you at a TAB or did you go to the racecourse?"

"I'm at Kilmore hun. Correct weight has just been announced. I'm going to get my winnings – $220 – and reinvest.

Which he did. As Pistachio's bankroll increased, his bets – always at fixed odds – got bigger and bigger. When the results of the first three races matched those on his newspaper's racing page, there was no doubt that the page he held in his hand was the real deal.

He cashed a couple of the early winning tickets – which put him in the black for life – and kept the others – including a quaddie ticket worth $8500 – safely tucked into his shirt pocket. After the eighth and last race of the day, Pistachio figured he had over $25,000 in cash stuffed into his pockets and another half-million dollars of winning tickets in his shirt pocket. He decided to cash those tickets at the TAB's head office in the city early the following week. They'd issue him a cheque or transfer the money straight into his bank account.

Pistachio didn't have a TAB account which would allow him to place bets using his phone. "Too much temptation," he often said. Several of his mates had either the TAB or Sportsbet ap and one or two were up to their eyeballs in debt since it took all of five seconds to make a bet. Pistachio placed his bets in person or not at all.

On the walk back to his car Pistachio was so deep in thought he didn't realise that he was being followed by a couple of undesirables who had not had the luxury of knowing the winners before the races were run. Eddie "Bean Pole" Corrochio and Jimmy "Meatballs" Angelini had cashed just three tickets between them on the day and had kept an eye on Pistachio, who had done his best to blend in with the small crowd. He hadn't carried on like a loon when he won but Corrochio and Angelini noticed Pistachio's frequent trips to the windows to cash his tickets and not once did they see him toss away a losing one.

"This guy is either the best handicapper I've ever seen, or he's got some inside info," Corrochio said to Angelini after the fourth race. "He's flush with cash and being by himself he'll be an easy mark."

"We'll roll him after the last," Angelini said. "But not here. Too many cameras. You drive up ahead of him – like we did to that bloke last month near Moonee Valley – and I'll give him a little tap from behind.

Corrochio got into his car and Angelini his. Pistachio got into his late model dark Toyota Camry and started to move toward the exit onto East St. Corrochio saw Pistachio's left indicator go on and sped up to get in front of him. Angelini followed in his Mitsubishi and got behind Pistachio. At the second traffic light they came to, Corrochio abruptly stopped as the light turned amber and then red. Pistachio had to slam on his brakes to avoid hitting Corrochio's car but was jolted forward by a knock from the car behind him. When Angelini got out of his Mitsubishi to examine the damage – a busted taillight and a few scratches – Pistachio did the same.

"Sorry mate," Angelini said. "I must not have been paying attention."

"It's not your fault. It was the guy in front of me. He stopped suddenly so I had to do the same to avoid running up his bum."

"Let's settle this like gentleman," Angelini said. "Empty your pockets."

"What?"

"I said empty your pockets."

"I'm not paying you. You ran into me."

Angelini opened his jacket wide enough for Pistachio to see he had a gun tucked into his waistband.

"Hand your winnings over."

Pistachio looked at Angelini, who was bigger than he was, and took notice of the driver from the car in front of him, who had gotten out of his car and joined the discussion. He was as tall as an AFL behind post and wider than a Collingwood supporter. Pistachio was hemmed in and had no choice but to do as Angelini asked.

He took the large wad of bills he had in his front left pocket and handed them over.

"The rest of it mate," barked the goalpost.

As Pistachio reached into his right pocket the light turned green. The drivers of the cars behind them began to lean on their horns. "Hey arseholes, move those pieces of shit out of the way," one driver shouted from the cab of his truck.

The crack drew Angelini's attention. "Who the fuck said that?" he said turning around. Corrochio grabbed Angelini by the shoulder. "Jimmy," he calmly said. "Let it go. We've got what we wanted. Let's get outta here."

Pistachio had the same idea and bolted across the street to the safety of a service station on the corner before Angelini and Corrochio realised he was gone.

The two hopped in Angelini's Mitsubishi. Angelini backed up, swerved around Pistachio's car and the one Corrochio had stolen several days ago in Melbourne, ran the red light and sped away.

Pistachio watched the thieves peel away while hiding behind a display of motor oil. His heart was thumping so loudly he thought it was going to burst out of his chest. His legs felt like jelly, and he was barely able to catch his breath. "Call triple zero for me, will you?" he said to someone waiting in line to pay for his petrol. "I was just robbed at gunpoint."

Pistachio checked his pockets as his breathing and heart rate returned to normal. More than half of his winnings were gone, but luckily not the racing page which was stuffed into his right-hand pocket. The other copy was in his jacket pocket. He felt his shirt pocket. His winning tickets were safe.

Pistachio grabbed a bottle of water from a cooler, left a $2 coin on the service station's front counter and drank half of it. He slowly walked across the busy street to his car. He got in, turned on the car's hazard lights, grabbed his phone from the storage compartment of the centre console where he left it and pressed Sarah's number. As he did, a cop car pulled up behind him.

Ninety minutes later Pistachio was finally on his way home. It was dark and he crawled along in peak-hour traffic. It was nearly 7pm when it dawned on him that the meeting at Pakenham had started an hour ago. Three of the eight races had already been run. He spotted a service station up ahead, signalled and parked far away from the bowsers.

He picked up his phone and punched in the words, *Where is the nearest TAB?*

There was one at a pub in Craigieburn, 15ks away. "I can make it there in time for the fourth."

He arrived at the pub at 7:22, went straight to the TAB, checked his racing page and using one of the TAB's automated betting machines, placed a large win bet at the fixed odds of $11.40 on Up All Night. It saluted but this time Pistachio did not cash the ticket. *No need to bring any attention to myself*, he thought.

He ordered a meal at the bar and rang Sarah.

"You're where?" she asked. "At a TAB? In Craigieburn? Even after what happened earlier?"

"Yes, yes and yes," he said.

"This is a once in a lifetime thing honey. I'm going to grab a quick bite, put the rest of the bets on and head home." He checked his watch. "See you about 9:15. Yes, I'll be careful."

While he waited for his meal Pistachio put his quaddie bet on – which was going to pay a healthy $2552 – and several, exacta, trifecta, first four and win bets. He placed all the tickets in the safety of his shirt pocket. Unless some joker barged in demanding to launder everyone's shirts, he figured the tickets were safe.

The young bartender placed Pistachio's burger, chips and salad on his table meant for four and asked him if he wanted another beer. "Make it a Coke please. I'm driving."

"I couldn't help notice you put a few bets on," the bartender said when he returned.

"Yeah, to watch later when I get home."

"If there anything you like? I've been on a bit of a losing streak."

Pistachio carefully looked him over. He had an honest face and didn't see a gun, so he decided to share his good fortune. It could help his karma.

"It's just a hunch but in the quaddie at Pakenham I like the 7, 6, 9 and 1."

"You're not backing anything else? Just singling out one horse in each race?"

"Just the one mate."

"You're that confident?"

Pistachio smiled for the first time in several hours. "I am."

The Switch

The brass nameplate on my office door reads Brodie Ganderson. I'm one of the associates at the Melbourne law firm of Donaldson, Chafee and Howe. You might have seen our ads on TV. They run mostly during the day. They're corny but very, effective. We have one gal who's permanently assigned to answer the flood of calls that come in. If I had a dollar every time I've heard Lisa Roland say "Donaldson, Chafee and Howe, please hold," I'd be on a beach in Port Douglas with an Esky full of cold ones six months a year.

I've just seen one of the ads. Why it's airing during the last round of the Masters Golf Tournament and not during one of the morning chat shows is something I'll bring up at our weekly meeting.

I won't be in until sometime after 11 today. Watching the final round of The Masters is something I do every year. The golf tournament, one of the four majors, takes place at the end of March or the beginning of April. Every few years the tournament ends on Easter Sunday in the US and Easter Monday here. Not so today, meaning I'll get dressed during the ad breaks and head out the door as soon as the green jacket is presented to the winner. Yeah, I could record it and watch it when I get home tonight but I'm not much for watching things after the results are known.

I plan to catch up with my golfing buddies after work where we'll dissect the last round over drinks and plan our next outing which could be this weekend at one of the sand belt courses if the weather stays mild. The only problem is that the weekend after The Masters everybody and his mother thinks they're Tiger Woods and wants a tee time.

"We really should go down there one year, see Augusta National in all its glory," Dave "Five Iron" Simmons says as he plants a jug of beer on our table at a watering hole near the Crown Casino. It's within walking distance of where we all work and just a short walk from the trams and trains which will take us home. Sitting to my right is Dom Williams and to my left Ryan "Bubba" Watson.

"I'd never be able to get away," Watson says. "Neither would I," Williams adds. "I'm sure my wife would like to get rid of me for two weeks, but it would cost an absolute fortune and I couldn't afford it."

"Pull your kids out of those private schools of theirs. Then you'd be able to afford it." Simmons says. "You must be chucking away 40 grand a year."

"Closer to 50."

"You're paying 50 grand a year for private schools? Un-fucking-believable. Nothing wrong with state schools if you ask me. My son goes to one."

"My wife insists the kids go to private schools," says Williams. "That's where her salary goes."

I look at Simmons. "Guess it would be just the two of us," I say.

"Separate rooms," he replies.

"I wouldn't dream of coming between you and your five iron mate."

That night, after some reasonably decent Thai takeaway, I do a little online homework on The Masters; how to get tickets, the nearby hotels, airfares. Unlike Dom, I'm able to afford it. I live on my own, have no steady girlfriend and there are no kids asking me to bring home pizza, borrow my iPad or do their homework for them.

Golf has been my partner the past few months and it turns out I am just as bad with a club in my hands as I am at keeping a relationship going. My handicap is 22 or 20 less than my age. My last girlfriend said I didn't pay enough attention to her or do things she wanted to do. I mean, what's wrong with golf? You're outside, getting exercise, have a chance to win a side bet or two, break for lunch and a beer and then down another couple of cold ones in the clubhouse after finishing the back nine.

It's also where scorecards are added up and side bets settled, and lately that part of the day has not been pretty. I haven't broken 95 in two months. My drives are shit, my iron play stinks, and I haven't sunk a putt longer than 20 feet since Augusta National Tiger-proofed the finest course in the world 20 years ago. It's now got more length than a pair of jeans sold at Kmart.

Dom says I need to learn to separate work from my private life and he's probably right. I'm trying to keep an 18-year-old from spending the next three-to-five years of his life at a run-down, violence and gang-infested juvenile correction facility for an armed robbery I'm sure he didn't commit and it's starting to get to me a bit.

Charlie Butler's trial starts the week after next and I have to say it's not looking good for him. A witness I was counting on suddenly decided against testifying, leaving me without someone to back up my client's whereabouts.

Charlie Butler was simply at the wrong place at the wrong time when a fast-food outlet several kilometres away from his home was robbed at knifepoint by two teenagers in hoodies.

Like most his age, Butler was also wearing a hoodie on the fresh Autumn night, but he was attempting to ward off the chill in the air and not trying to hide his face from the restaurant's staff and security cameras.

The staff of six were scared shitless when the two thugs walked into the restaurant, drew their knives, and asked for all the money in the tills. When the coppers arrived, all the customers in the joint ran off including my witness. They even took their burgers, fries, and shakes with them. That's as good an advertisement for a business as you'll ever see.

My client, who was wearing the same dark-coloured hoodie as the robbers, wasn't as quick and was thrown to the ground and cuffed. One copper picked up a discarded knife 10 metres away. "I reckon this belongs to you mate," he said.

Several staff members slowly came outside to watch the proceedings and were told by senior sergeant Bill Robinson that one of the likely perps was in custody.

"Thank goodness. They were wearing hoodies and showed us knives. One spoke, the other pointed to the cash draw," 17-year-old cashier Wanda Sendowski told the senior sergeant.

"See the lad we have cuffed? That one of the two?" Robinson asked the Year 11 student.

Butler was now on his feet, his hands cuffed behind him. Wanda Sendowski gave him the once over. "I'm pretty sure that's him. I'll testify too. This is the third time we've been robbed this year. This is officially my last shift. I'm going to work at Big W. Nobody is going in there with knives looking to rob the place."

Unfortunately for Butler, the restaurant's security cameras were not functioning properly. Had they been he would have immediately been cleared. Instead, he was looking at a long stretch away from home even though he had no prior record and was a decent student.

"It's going to be your word against the girl's, Charlie," I told him and his parents in my office 10 days later. His mum and dad had hired us after seeing one of our television ads.

"What about the fingerprints on the knife? They can't be Charlie's," Walter Butler asked. His wife nodded her head as he talked.

I explained to Charlie and his parents that the knife found near him was mishandled by a junior constable and that any prints on the knife were gone.

"Can't the case be dropped because of that?" Walter Butler asked.

"In most cases, yes. But the prosecution has a restaurant employee who is going to testify that it was Charlie who approached the counter."

Charlie Butler stood up. "That is absolute bullshit. I was just having a burger with Frankie. He'll vouch for me."

"I'm afraid he won't," I told the Butlers. "As you may know he's been in trouble before and is denying that he was there that night. He said he was home studying, and his parents are backing up his alibi."

"Frankie study? He's never studied for anything as long as I've known him. He cheats on every test he takes."

"Maybe so but he's not the one who's going to be on trial."

"This is a fucking nightmare," Walter Butler asked. "We're paying your firm enough money. Can you get a jury to believe Charlie? What are his chances?"

"That depends," I told them. A yellow legal pad filled with notes was in front of me. "We have options."

"What are they?" Walter Butler asked.

Charlie Butler had no prior arrests and had never been in trouble with the cops. Had he not celebrated his 18th birthday two weeks before the robbery, he would have been tried in Magistrates Court and had his case heard by a judge. His sentence, if the judge had found him guilty, would have been for no more than a year.

I had gotten Charlie out on bail and was quietly confident I could convince a jury that he was innocent. However, to do that I'd have to convince the same jury that the cashier had mistaken Charlie for one of the real culprits. Cross examining a 17-year-old girl would be tricky at best especially if she broke down on the stand. A jury would be easily swayed by a teary-eyed girl traumatised by an armed robbery. The prosecution would bolster its case by pointing out that she hadn't been the same since, had missed school, been unable to work. I'll argue that the prosecution had ruined the lone piece of evidence – the knife – which could clear Charlie and that the lack of security camera vision was the fault of the restaurant.

"My advice is to fight the case in court. I'd advise against a plea bargain which would be an admission of guilt."

"Would a plea bargain keep my son out of jail?" Walter Butler asked.

"Depends on the judge. He'd been looking at either six months in jail and a fine, or some sort of community service and a fine."

"Give us a minute, will you please?" Walter Butler asked me.

I left the conference room and stood outside while the Butlers talked things over.

Five minutes later Walter Butler opened the door and motioned for me to come back in.

"We're going to fight this in court. No son of ours would commit a robbery. Charlie told us he's innocent and we believe him," he said.

"Good. I'll let you know when Charlie's next court appearance is. It will be just a formality, to organise a trial date. In the meantime, I'll get to work on his defence."

I shook hands with Charlie and his mum and dad and showed them out.

By the time Charlie's case was heard a few weeks later I had spent north of $6000 on tickets for next year's Masters Golf Tournament from a reputable travel agency which also handled flights, accommodation, and a hire car. Five Iron Simmons shelled out the same amount.

We convinced ourselves it was worth it by telling each other it was a once in a lifetime experience. It would turn out to be a life-changing experience for one of us.

Charlie's trial lasted three days. On the last day I did my best to plant a seed of doubt in the jury's mind. "Without any security camera footage and without his fingerprints on the weapon recovered you cannot send this fine young man, who has never been in trouble before, to prison," I told the seven men and five women chosen to decide his fate.

I pointed to Charlie as I said that. He looked more like a young associate than a defendant in his sharp suit and tie. His parents sat directly behind us. All the lead prosecutor had was 17-year-old cashier Wanda Sendowski's testimony. She repeatedly cried on the stand and when I glanced at the jury, I sensed several believed her.

Under cross examination I got her to admit that she wasn't 100 percent sure it was Charlie Butler who waved a knife at her and demanded money.

I liked my chances when the case went to the jury but as the hours passed, I began to have doubts.

Finally, on a late Thursday afternoon, after seven hours of deliberation, the jury returned a verdict of not guilty. Charlie Butler was free to go. His parents hugged each other and then their son. Each shook my hand. Walter Butler patted me on the back. "Thank you, Mr Ganderson," he said.

I put my papers in my briefcase and caught a tram back to the office. "It was never in doubt," I jokingly told the partners on my return.

There was a wrongful death case waiting on my desk which I got stuck into the next morning. It dragged on for months, but we got the verdict we wanted and a large portion of a multi-million-dollar settlement. Following that win I worked with two others on a high-profile divorce involving a former AFL footballer which made headlines due to the kinky sex lives he and his wife indulged in. One photo which made the rounds on social media featured an interchange bench of nude and very busty women. As far as we were able to ascertain, they came on and off the bench at five-minute intervals to join the footballer and his wife on a bed the size of a goal square. When the wife found out her husband was poking a few through the big sticks without her being present, she didn't get even, she called our firm to as she put it "fuck him up the arse."

We immediately decided to represent her – the publicity it gave us was better than a hundred of our TV ads – and while she didn't get all of what she wanted – house, BMW, boat, shares in two racehorses, and a couple of million bucks – she got plenty and would never have to work again in her life. Not that she had ever worked before unless you call dressing up for Brownlow Medal night and the spring racing carnival work.

Before you knew it, the Christmas holidays were upon us. Since Donaldson, Chafee and Howe were having a very profitable year, the office Christmas party was a lavish sit-down dinner and booze-filled affair with enough toasts to knock a sailor on his arse. We're a pretty close-knit group, and unlike other companies no one ever complains about a drunken pass or a couple of off-colour remarks at a social event. At the office however, we behave like thorough professionals.

Three other companies held their Christmas parties at the same venue as ours, albeit in different ballrooms. The liveliest ballroom was ours since we had a DJ who started pumping out tunes right after dessert was served. A well-known insurance company in the ballroom next to ours lived up to its stuffy reputation by hiring a string quartet. About half of its staff wound up in our ballroom when the quartet put down its bows and took a break.

I had a few drinks and danced around a bit with a very attractive young woman from the insurance firm who had a pair of legs longer than an AFL goalpost. I didn't even know her name until we got in a cab together and went back to her place for a nightcap. She should have sued me for non-compliance after I fell asleep in her bed without even issuing a subpoena.

She was a good sport about it all the next morning. We had a cup of coffee and toast, and all was fine until I told her I was 42 years old.

She had the same look on her face an archaeologist has when finding something on a dig in the desert that's 1000 years old.

She stood up, leaving her cup on the kitchen table. "Forty-two? My dad is 46."

"C'mon. Forty-two isn't that old," I pleaded. "At my last check-up my doctor told me I had the body of a 41-year-old."

"Is that supposed to be funny?"

"I thought it was. How old are you Kylie?"

She put her hand on her hips. "Twenty-three."

I did the math. I had to admit a 19-year age gap could be considered a game-breaker by some.

"I bet you're not even on Instagram," she said "And you probably play golf all the time like my dad."

I was buried deep in a bunker and needed a miracle to get out of it. I countered with "not all the time, just on the weekends."

Splash! From the bunker right into the water.

"I think you should leave," Kylie said.

"You mean we're not going to?" I asked as I moved my eyebrows up and down.

"No grandpa. We are not."

Angry face and all, and at 10 in the morning with no make-up, standing there in just a nightshirt was as pretty a sight as I had even seen, including Amen Corner at Augusta National.

"Not even a couple of holes?"

"Keep your putter in your pants mate."

I grabbed my shoes, checked my pockets to make sure I had everything I came in with and walked to the door. She held it open and slammed it behind me.

Ten weeks later Dave "Five Iron" Simmons and I are at Melbourne's Tullamarine Airport waiting for our non-stop flight to Dallas-Fort Worth in Texas. We agreed to fly economy class so we could spend every dollar we have on the ground. I've got a couple of sportswriter Dan Jenkins' finest novels in my carry-on bag to pass the time on the 17-hour plus flight. The couple of laughs per page make the marathon flight bearable. It's the second longest flight Qantas offers; only the non-stop flight from Perth to London is longer. Thankfully there was an empty seat between me and Five Iron. At one point he was able to grind out a few hours of sleep. I was up for nearly the entire flight. I can do a lot of things but sleeping on a plane is not one of them.

Jenkins hadn't missed a major in over 50 years. His recent passing ended the streak.

Five Iron and I will be attending our first. I'm guessing Jenkins used to fly into Augusta on a private plane and stayed at one of Augusta's better hotels.

Dave and I were lucky enough to breeze through customs at Dallas-Fort Worth but had to claim our bags and then re-check them for the flight into Hartsfield Airport in Atlanta which I later learned is the busiest airport in the US.

Five Iron snacked on a piece of undistinguishable meat stuffed in a roll which was buried in barbecue sauce before we boarded our flight to Atlanta. He lapped up the dripping brown sauce like a hungry dog attacking its morning food bowl. When I asked a very large fellow wearing a 10-gallon hat behind the counter for the pulled pork roll but without the barbecue sauce he looked at me like I was from Neptune. "I've got a dicky stomach mate," I told him.

"You got a what?"

"Stomach issues."

"Suit yourself but you're missing the best part of the meal champ."

Americans call each other champ, chief or motherfucker the way we call each other mate.

I handed him a $20 note to pay for the roll and Diet Coke but didn't realise it was an Aussie note until he had it in his greasy hands.

"What the hell is this? Monopoly money?" he asked. "We don't take this plastic shit," he said handing it back to me. "Greenbacks only champ."

"My mistake mate, I've got US dollars on me."

I took out my wallet and gave him a $US20 note. He gave me back four singles (dollar bills) and a shitload of coins.

The roll wasn't half bad. Five Iron seemed to enjoy his. There was so much sauce on his chin he looked like he had grown a beard overnight. He looked around for a toilet to wash it all off. "There must be an art to eating this stuff," he said before wandering off.

"Meet you at the boarding gate," I hollered to him.

I spotted a newsagent and bought the *Dallas Morning News*, a broadsheet paper serving the Dallas-Fort Worth Area. Americans like everything on the big side; food, drink and their own waistlines. I doubt I'll arrive home with my 34-inch waistline intact.

However, their newspapers are as skinny as a supermodel. It's like half the thing is missing. There's no width to them. They're about a third of the size of *The Australian*.

I take a seat at the boarding gate. We've got nearly an hour to wait before we can board. The flight is supposedly fully booked but only half the seats at the gate are taken. I put my carry-on bag between my legs and turn to the sports section. It's Monday and featured prominently among the NBA basketball, pre-season baseball, ice hockey stories and a yarn on the upcoming NFL draft and who the Cowboys should pick, is a large spread on The Masters. The weather forecast for Augusta National catches my eye. Sunny skies for the rest of the week, temperatures in the mid-70s or about 23° Celsius. Perfect. One of the club's greenskeepers says the rain which has fallen over the past few weeks has the course in pristine condition.

I look up, see Five Iron and wave to catch his attention. He takes the seat next to me. "What's making news?" he asks.

"Some golf tournament in Georgia we happen to be going to."

Neither one of us are big on high-fives, but on this occasion, we raise our hands and slap them together.

Dave is not the reader I am. He prefers to listen to podcasts on his iPhone. But he picks up the news section of the *Dallas Morning News* out of curiosity and opens it. He elbows me gently in the ribs. "What the fuck is this? Where's the rest of the paper?" he asks.

"That's just what I said."

"It's like a mini golf course." He turns a few pages. "I can't read this."

He puts it down and checks his phone.

"But when you're done with the sports section let me have a squiz, okay?"

The 90-minute flight to Atlanta leaves on time. We're seated side-by-side and before we even move onto the tarmac, two large blokes in front of us crack open a couple of beers and recline their seats so far back that they're practically in our laps. "Should I say something?" I ask Dave.

"Nah. One of the flight attendants will ask them to put their seats back in the true position before we take off."

Just as he says that a stunning woman with short blonde hair in a snappy tailored uniform appears and politely asks the two blokes to put their seats into the upright position.

"Sure honey, whatever you say," one replies.

"Think she's a member of that mile-high club?" his mate asks after she leaves.

"Without a doubt. This guy I know who works on the ground says it a virtual fuckfest at 37,000 feet with them and the pilots."

"She looks a little bit like your first wife, don't she Dwayne?"

Dwayne Hayes gives the flight attendant a look that the first Mrs Hayes didn't particularly care for. It's the same look he has when he's about to tuck into an extra-large bucket of the Colonel's finest.

"Anita never looked that good in her life," Hayes tells Billy Joe Dupree. "You agree?"

"I reckon Anita is prettier," Dupree says.

"You always did have a soft spot for Anita, didn't you? You can tell me."

"You wouldn't be wrong Dwayne," Dupree says, draining the beer he deftly hid from the flight attendant.

"You didn't sleep with her Billy Joe? Did you?"

Dupree didn't say a word.

"Why you son of a bitch. You fucked my wife. I oughta lay you out right here."

"It was after you two split up. I was comforting her."

"Let's see how comfortable this feels," Dwayne Hayes said. He reared back and slugged Billy Joe Dupree square in the jaw with a textbook right hand. Dupree's fastened seat belt was the only thing which kept him from tumbling out of his seat into the aisle. Dupree shook off the blow, unfastened his seat belt, stood up and started to pummel the larger Hayes with left and right hands. People all around started screaming and when the two were finally pried apart by several male flight attendants there was a fair bit of blood on Hayes's Dallas Cowboys t-shirt and a few less teeth in his mouth. Dave and I were already out of our seats and had backed away by the time Dupree went all Apollo Creed on Hayes's face.

Both combatants were held down by several flight attendants and passengers, and cuffed by cops who boarded the flight like Israeli commandos in *Raid on Entebbe*. All around them passengers were filming the brouhaha on their phones. We saw footage of the incident later that night in our motel room. Hayes and Dupree were escorted off the plane and taken away by the coppers. Hayes asked one of the arresting officers if he could be taken to a dentist first. He was told to do something to himself which is physically impossible.

While the crew removed the belongings of Hayes and Dupree from the plane, Dave and I reclaimed our seats just in time to hear the pilot announce that there would be a "slight delay" due to what he called a "pre-flight altercation".

We finally took off 45 minutes late and arrived in Atlanta mid-afternoon. We grabbed our luggage from baggage claim, got our rental car without a hassle and took off for Atlanta.

Dave drove since he was more awake than me. He did alright, considering it was his first time driving on the right-hand side of the road. The only problem was the windshield wipers kept going on every time we needed to make a turn.

It took us about two and a half hours to get to the La Quinta Inn, one of the many chain hotels in the area. It was a little run down but just an iron shot from Augusta National.

Our room had a balcony and the two single beds which we had asked for. The bathroom was larger than most motel offerings and cleaner too. The only issue for me was the globes in the bedside lamps which hardly gave off any light. I asked for a stronger globe from a young fellow at the main desk before we went out for dinner.

"A globe? What do you mean?" he asked in an accent I could not make out.

"A light bulb," I answered pointing to a lamp in the lobby.

"Why do you need a new light bulb? The one in the room works, yes?"

"Yes, it works mate, but it's too dim. I need a stronger globe so I can read at night. Do you have one?" I politely asked.

"I go look. One moment."

Two minutes later he returned with a light bulb in his hands. He handed it to me.

"That's three dollars."

"You're charging me for a light bulb?"

"More light, more power, higher price," I was told.

I checked the wattage of the bulb. Seventy-five watts. The bulb in the room was 40 watts. It would do. I reluctantly handed over three singles, walked across the lobby and up a couple of flights of stairs to our room. We were on the top floor of the three-storey building, and I had earlier decided I would walk as much as possible to work off the extra calories I'd be putting on over the next week. For me, the motel's elevator was off limits.

For some unexplained reason our tickets did not include the par three tournament the day before the Masters begins so we spent the next two days driving around the city of Augusta, lounging in the sun by the La Quinta Inn's pool – never to be the training pool of an Olympic champion – and getting over our jet lag. On Wednesday night we went to the Longhorn Steakhouse for dinner. Just about everyone in the place, including the staff, was decked out in golf apparel. I'd have clad the waiters and waitresses in caddie outfits.

"No, you shouldn't tackle the steak from left to right. Aim for the right-hand side and work your knife and fork to the centre. You'll need more butter on your jacket potato. Try two more packets," they'd tell diners.

While we waited for our steaks Dave grabbed us a couple of Budweisers from the bar. The King of Beers it's called. The bottles of Budweiser were cold, but the beer was not to our liking.

"How can the Yanks drink this? It's bloody awful," Dave grimaced as he put the beer down. "I can't finish this."

I agreed.

"Let me see what else they have," I said making my way to the bar.

I returned with two bottles of Miller just as our steaks arrived. They were served just as we had asked, medium-well for me and well-done done for Dave. The steaks were fine, the Millers passable. Dave went back to the bar and returned with two bottles of Coors.

"Third time lucky," I said as we lifted the bottles to our lips.

Coors got a pass mark from each of us.

The tournament kicked off at 7am the next morning. We grabbed a quick breakfast at the motel – it was part of our package – and rocked up to Augusta National just after 8am. It was a beautiful sunny morning with barely a hint of wind – perfect conditions for those with a morning tee time.

We caught a shuttle bus from the motel to Augusta's tree-lined front entrance. It was like entering the world's finest botanical garden. We walked past the clubhouse and saw three-time Masters winner Rich Marshall and someone we did not recognise returning from the practice tees. We later learned it was an amateur Marshall had been paired with for the opening round. They had an 8:45am tee time. I hadn't asked anyone for an autograph since I was in high school, but decided I would ask the tall leftie to sign my cap. He couldn't have been any nicer. He even used his own pen since a pen was the last thing I thought I would need.

"You guys look a little lost," Marshall said as he signed my cap. "First time here?"

"It is."

"What do you think?"

"Amazing, just amazing," we said in unison.

He handed me back my cap. I shook his large hand. As I did, I felt a bit of static electricity pass from his hand to mine. He didn't look like he had felt a thing although a cell phone in his golf bag rang.

"Sorry fellas," he said looking at the name of the caller. "Gotta take this."

Augusta National is one of the few remaining places on the planet where mobile phones are strictly prohibited. Marshals enforce the rule, so we left our phones back at the motel. It was actually enjoyable to be without them. No text messages, no emails. We were able to concentrate fully on the golf. We walked to the first tee which was lined with hundreds of people. Greg Garcia, Ian Powter and Bubba Wilson each took a few practice swings and sent perfect drives down the fairway.

I glanced at my watch. It was 8:40. Marshall, amateur Riley Barnett, and Derek Johannson were up next. Barnett, a 19-year-old baby-faced college kid, looked like Marshall's son as they walked to the tee. Barnett was announced to the crowd first. I'd have been so nervous hitting my first ball at The Masters that I would have missed it entirely. But he touched his cap to acknowledge the crowd and then calmly drove his ball straight down the fairway. I lost sight of it, but Barnett and his caddie were happy with his shot and backed away from the tee.

Johannson was introduced to the patrons and followed with a shot straight down the fairway.

From an unseen speaker we then heard the following:

"Now stepping up to the first tee, from Scottsdale, Arizona, please welcome three-time Masters champion Rich Marshall.

Always the showman, Marshall doffed his cap to the applause of the crowd, took two practice swings and then stepped to the tee. The crowd fell silent as Marshall rocked back and forth, swung his driver back and made contact. All eyes looked up, but they should have been looking down because the ball barely got airborne. It skidded off the grass and travelled all of 100 feet. The crowd gasped. Marshall looked at his driver to see if something was wrong with it. There wasn't.

"What the fuck?" he said loud enough for everyone to hear. *I haven't flubbed a shot like that since I was eight,* he said to himself. The miss-hit was later replayed over and over around the world. The on-course

CBS television commentators did their best to explain what happened as Marshall, Barnett and Johannson walked off the tee.

Shaking his head, Marshall brushed off his caddie and walked by himself to where his ball had rolled. He was on the edge of the fairway with a good lie. He took a three iron from his bag and took several practice swings as a crowd built behind him. A cameraman hustled back up the fairway and got in position less than 20 feet away from the Arizonan. Marshals held up their quiet please signs to the talkative crowd. Marshall stepped away from the ball until the noise subsided.

When he was comfortable, he again approached his Titleist. He took a couple of practice swings, made sure his footing was just right, drew back his club and struck the ball solidly. But again, it failed to travel more than 100 yards. He was still more than 200 yards from the green on the Par 4 hole.

Dave and I looked at each other in disbelief. "He's playing like you mate. He'll be out of contention before he hits the back nine," Dave said.

Barnett's second shot landed at the edge of the green. A par was in the offing.

It took two more shots for Marshall to reach the green. None of his four shots had gotten more than 50 feet in the air. By the time Marshall sank his fourth putt for a quadruple bogey, he was trending on Twitter.

Marshall walked to the par 5, 575-yard second hole by himself. As word of Marshall's troubles got around the course, a crowd 30 and 40 deep converged on the second tee.

The hundreds of reporters in the media centre had their eyes glued to a pair of big screen TVs mounted on a wall at the front of the building.

Showing no signs of nervousness, Barnett again nailed his drive straight down the fairway. All eyes were now on Marshall. He grabbed a driver out of his bag, planted his tee, placed his Titleist on it and stepped back. He took a few deep breaths and imagined himself back on the practice tees. He took his cap off, wiped a few beads of sweat from his forehead and again approached the ball. He took a couple of practice swings and was set. The crowd fell completely silent. He brought his driver back and again failed to strike the ball cleanly. It travelled a little further than his drive on the first hole, but the shot was one of a weekend duffer, not a professional with tens of millions of dollars in prize money in the bank.

Marshall threw down his club, walked off the course and straight into the clubhouse.

"Get me the fuck out of here," he screamed at one of the clubhouse attendants.

A couple of camera crews chased Marshall into the clubhouse but that was as far as they got. Marshall left the course via a side entrance hiding in the back seat of a car driven by Eddie Muso, who dropped him off at the large house he was renting in one of Augusta's finest suburbs. Marshall punched in the gate's security code, made sure it closed behind him and walked straight to the fridge where he pulled out a beer. He was the only one at home. His wife and kids were at the course. *I'll ring them as soon as I can sort things out*, he thought. Marshall sat down in a large chair and drained the beer in a just a few gulps. He got up and opened the door to an expansive backyard where earlier in the week he had set up a net to hit balls into. He took a driver from an extra bag of clubs he carted around, placed a ball on a tee and again miss-hit it. "What the fuck is going on," he screamed over the sound of the swimming pool pump. He emptied a full bucket of balls onto a piece of astro turf, just like the kind one finds at driving ranges, took a five iron from his bag, and started hitting balls into the net. Every single shot was crap. He walked to a makeshift putting green, took his putter out and missed every single putt more than five feet from the hole. "Shit," he hollered.

Back at Augusta National the course was buzzing with the news of Marshall's withdrawal.

Five Iron and I joined the pilgrimage to Amen Corner which comprises holes 11, 12 and 13 and is said to be the place where Masters prayers are answered and ignored, and green jackets won and lost. Rae's Creek flows in front of the 12th green and behind the 11th green. A tributary runs up the left side of the 13th fairway and in front of the greens. Even the best high-definition television set in the world cannot capture Amen Corner's beauty. The trees, bushes and shrubbery are beautiful, and give off a scent which should be bottled. The last time I smelled something so sweet I was sitting behind Sarah Devaney in English class in high school. The sounds of the birds and the flowing water of the creek add to the place's beauty. Who knows how many people have scattered the ashes of their loved ones here over the years? I'm guessing tens of thousands. There is not a better resting place. Try and name one. Go on. Cable Beach? No. Cradle Mountain? No. The Blue Mountains? No. The Daintree? No. The Grand Canyon? Maybe.

Back at Marshall's rented home, a large pack of reporters and cameramen gathered outside the security gate. It looked like a scene outside Buckingham Palace where reporters wait to find out the details of a royal birth. Ordinarily the press leaves the golfers alone after their on-course press conferences. Some dine and drink at the same restaurants in the evening, but any talk is purely social, and all comments are off the record.

Hearing the commotion, Marshall walked to a window overlooking the front of the house and gently peeled back the curtains. "Shit. Look at that mob. How the fuck did they find me so quickly?" Ten minutes later a drone began flying over the house, sending live pictures back to one of the local TV stations. "This is insane. If that drone belongs to the mob at ESPN, I'm never going to do another interview with the fuckers. I better ring Deidre and tell her to stay away."

Deidre is Marshall's wife of 22 years and the mother of their three teenage children. Picking up his cell phone he saw over 60 text messages from friends, fellow players and reporters who all want to know what happened on those first two holes.

"What's going on Rich?" Deidre asked when she answered her phone.

"I have no idea hun but stay away from the house for now, okay? There are a ton of reporters at the front gate."

"What happened out on the course?"

"I don't know. I'm trying to figure it out myself."

"Do you feel okay? Are you sick?"

"I'm fine Deidre, really. Maybe I can tell the press I had a case of food poisoning or something. Stay at the course. I'll get back to you soon."

After spending nine hours at Augusta and with tickets for the next three days, Dave and I decided to call it a day even though a third of the field was still on the course. Riley Barnett, the young amateur who teed off with Marshall, was safely in the clubhouse with a five under 67 and was a good bet to make the cut when the field of 100 was halved after round two.

Facing the press after shooting a 67 in his first lap around Augusta would have been daunting enough for anyone. The fact that he and Johannson played the last 16 holes without Marshall had Riley feeling like a presidential press secretary. The questions came at him as quick as a Nolan Ryan fastball as cameras flashed in his face.

"Did Rich say anything to you?"

"Is he ill?"

"Have you ever walked off a course?"

"No, no and no," Barnett said.

"Care to elaborate?"

"No."

Johannson was the next to face the media.

"Rich's a pro, he'll bounce back. It was just one of those things."

"No, he never said anything to me."

The same questions kept coming so Johannson put his hands up, got out of the chair he was seated in and told the assembled media he would not be taking any more questions.

Much like those who want to have a kick of the footy after going to a game at the MCG, or have a hit after going to the cricket, Five Iron and I decided to go hit a few balls. It was just after five when one of the shuttle buses dropped us back at the La Quinta Inn. We did a quick Google search, got in the rental car, and drove to the Rolling Hills Driving Range, 15 minutes west of town.

We paid for a large bucket of balls and since we didn't have our clubs with us, we picked a few worn clubs from a large pile of drivers and irons and walked to two empty tees on the far right-hand side of the range. All the tees were under cover which shielded us from the strong late afternoon sun. I placed the bucket of balls between us, took a few practice swings with a driver, put a ball on the tee and was ready to go.

"Bet you a beer I outdrive you," Dave said.

"You're on. I'll hit first."

The feeling you get when perfectly striking a golf ball is like no other. It's better than the taste of a fine meal or top-shelf hootch, better than listening to Eric Clapton at a small club, better than seeing Niagara Falls and better than sex with Sarah Devaney, which I never experienced but dreamed about every night I was in high school and beyond.

My drive went straight down the fairway, kept gaining altitude, landed, and rolled until it came to rest near the 300-yard marker. I was just as shocked as Dave. Several of the other golfers on the range looked my way. I threw up my hands and said, "Lucky shot."

"I'd like to see you do that again," Dave said.

"So would I."

I teed up another ball, wrapped my hands around the same driver, brought the club back and again hit the ball perfectly. It travelled nearly as far as the first drive but carried a bit to the left. However, it would have landed safely on any fairway.

I was at a loss to explain my sudden turn-around in form. It was like a horse finishing last in his three prior starts bobbing up to win the Melbourne Cup.

"Let me see that club you're using?" Dave asked with his right arm outstretched.

I handed it to him.

He looked at it closely but found nothing unusual. "Let's see if the magic in this club is contagious."

Dave has a handicap of 12 and on a good day can drive a ball some 250 yards. His iron play and putting are the strengths of his game. He placed a ball on the tee, took a few practice swings and drove the ball about 200 yards down the fairway. He sliced his next shot. His third shot landed about 20 yards in front of his first.

"Well, it ain't the club," he said handing it back to me.

I teed up another shot and again knocked it out of sight.

Dave and I looked at each other. "When are you joining the tour?" he asked.

I put the driver aside, picked up a five iron and laid a ball on the fake green turf to the right of the tee. I struck the ball as sweet as a pro and lifted it 200 yards straight down the middle of the fairway. I tried a few pitches with a nine iron and left a half dozen balls within a foot of a flagstick which stood 100 yards away.

Dave stood beside me watching in disbelief.

"This has to be a dream. Because if it isn't, I'm going to qualifying school and getting my tour card," I told myself.

Later that night as I laid in bed I wondered if there was any connection between Marshall's disastrous first two holes and my sudden improvement. It took me a few days after The Masters ended to put the puzzle together. We were flying back to Dallas-Fort Worth, and my mind went back to the morning where Dave and I met Marshall. There was the brief handshake and the feeling of static electricity which came with it. Could I have acquired his golf skills and him mine as we shook hands? It was a ridiculous assumption, but it was all I had. How else to prove it? Should I shake the hand of a concert pianist? A great novelist? A surgeon?

Six months later ...

My handicap is officially one, an improvement of over 20 shots. Mine didn't come down gradually like everyone else's, it happened overnight. I've been on long service leave from Donaldson, Chafee and Howe for more than two months and I've spent my days playing every one of Melbourne's sand belt courses. I've broken par at all of them, including Royal Melbourne's west course, the toughest of the lot.

It's the first week of December. I've paid my $1870 entry fee and I'm standing near the first tee at Sandhurst's Club's north course in southeast Melbourne for Stage 1 of Section D's Qualifying School. I'm moments away from teeing off. Dave is standing next to me, clad in standard caddie gear. I'm not a superstitious sort, but I'm wearing the same cream-coloured pants and light blue polo shirt which I had on when I became the Jack Nicklaus of Augusta's Rolling Hills Driving Range.

In Scottsdale, Arizona, Rich Marshall is holed up in his mansion. He's been a virtual recluse since his Masters flop, which made the front page of every newspaper in the country. In the weeks after the Masters, golf experts picked apart each of his eight shots at the Masters in print and on television. They slowed down the videotape looking for a flaw, a nervous tick. Some pundits said he had a case of the yips. There was speculation that he was ill, on the drink, hooked on drugs. When he heard that he flung the remote control at the 60-inch living room TV so hard that it cracked the screen.

Marshall conferred with his swing coach, Shank Crosby.

They hit buckets of balls into nets strung up in the backyard of his home.

"I can't find anything wrong with your swing Rich. It's a fucking mystery. I'd suggest taking a rest and starting up again when you are mentally fresh."

At Deidre's urging Marshall made an appointment at the Mayo Clinic's Scottsdale facility to make sure there was nothing physically wrong with him. He went early one morning and slipped in and out without being seen which is no easy trick when you are 6-foot-4.

Several specialists ran numerous tests. Every single one came back negative.

"Physically you're fine Rich," Dr Andrew Maynard told him. "All your blood work is fine. Every cat scan we've done didn't turn up a thing. Neurologically there is nothing wrong. You're in perfect health actually."

"Then what could it be doctor? Is it a mental problem?"

"Could very well be. I'll giving you a referral to see Dr Boyd Mendelsohn. He's the best sports psychologist in the business. He's worked with golfers before. He's got an office in Los Angeles and another right here in Scottsdale where he works a couple of days a week. Give him a ring."

Dr Maynard handed him a referral and Dr Mendelsohn's card. Marshall shook his hand and walked out a back entrance and quickly strode to his car. He looked at the referral and Dr Mendelsohn's card, stuffed both into the BMW's glove box and drove home.

"How'd it go sweetheart?" Deidre asked when he arrived back home.

"I got a clean bill of health."

"That's wonderful."

"I guess. The top doctor who ran the tests suggested I see a sports psychologist."

"That's a good idea."

"You think?"

"Well, if there's nothing wrong with you physically, maybe it is a mental thing."

"Maybe it is."

Marshall rang Dr Mendelsohn's office later that morning and was told by his receptionist that there was a six-week waiting list to see the doctor. "Can't you squeeze me in?" Marshall pleaded.

"I'm sorry. The best I can do Mr Marshall is to put you on our cancellation list. If someone cancels, I'll ring you. In the meantime, I'll make that appointment for you in six weeks. Is there any day or time you prefer?"

"Any day is fine, I'm not going anywhere," a downcast Marshall said.

The three-time Masters winner didn't even go to the local supermarket anymore. He couldn't face the inevitable questions from shoppers, many of whom he called friends.

"What happened Rich?"

"When will we see you back?"

"How are you holding up champ?"

Then there were those who thought they had the answers to his woes.

"Change your grip Rich."

"Get a new caddie."

"My brother had the yips, changed his clubs and the yips disappeared overnight."

"Have you tried hypnosis? That's how I quit smoking."

Two days later, a Thursday, Marshall received a call from Dr Mendelsohn's office.

"We had a cancellation this morning. Can you come in tomorrow afternoon?" the receptionist asked.

Marshall was in Dr Mendelsohn's waiting room 45 minutes before his appointment.

I meet my playing partners in the Sandhurst clubhouse about 90 minutes before we tee off. I was handed a list of the morning's pairings and there in the 11:15am slot were the names Brodie Ganderson, Bob Corcoran and Reggie Cook. I look at it twice just to make sure. Yup. It's not a mistake, not a misprint, my name is there. Corcoran and Cook play off scratch as do most of the field so I'll need to play like Marshall to finish in the top 12 over the three days to advance to the final stage of qualifying school the following week at Moonah Links on the Mornington Peninsula.

There's a two-goal breeze blowing when our threesome tees off under sunny skies at 11:15 on the dot. You couldn't ask for better conditions. I'm expecting plenty of under par scores and the way I'm striking the ball of late I have a feeling I'll be in that group.

I am after the first 18 holes. I recovered from two bogeys on the front nine to shoot three under par on the day. It took a while for my nerves to settle down – hence the two bogeys – but once I got comfortable, I played well. Corcoran (one under) and Cook (even) also struggled early but played much better on the back nine.

"I never thought I would be so nervous," Corcoran, a 29-year-old landscaper, tells us in the clubhouse over a beer. Cook, two years older than me at 44, was making his eighth appearance at qualifying school. The accountant has never once cracked the top 12 needed to advance. "Two years ago, all I needed to do was par the last hole," he says. "I hooked my tee shot but was on the green in three. I had a 12-foot putt, 12 lousy feet for par, but blew it. The pressure got to me. The pros are right when they day that 90 percent of the game is mental. When you get right down to it all our games are pretty similar."

Corcoran and I nodded our heads in agreement. "I reckon that's why I played so poorly on the front nine. I needed time to settle. Maybe tomorrow it won't be so bad," Cook says.

I have an 8am tee time the next morning which I'm not so crazy about but it turns out to be much better than drawing an afternoon slot. The winds picked up considerably after lunch and few were able to break par. I'm at five under and in 10th place heading into the last round. Corcoran and Cook are each two shots off the top 12. "A few early birdies and I'll be right back in the picture," Corcoran says when I bump into him after lunch. I figure I'll need a round in the high 60s on the par 72 course to keep my spot in the top 12.

We've lucked out for Thursday's final round; there are sunny skies, and the wind is on the calm side. I'm paired with Hal Schneider (five under) and Dean Rosen (four under). The two have their game faces on; they barely even say hello at the first tee. Five Iron and I spent a good hour going over the pin placements and agree that a conservative approach is the best way to attack the course.

I'm even for the day when we make the turn and have slipped into a tie for 12th place with two others. If I don't make a few birdies on the back nine I'll be back at the offices of Donaldson, Chafee and Howe come Monday.

I grabbed a shot back by birdying the par 5 11th hole thanks to a wonderful approach shot which left with me with a six-foot putt. I scrambled to save par on the par three 15th hole. Schneider and Rosen each birdied it and I had to concede that they are in another league. But then again this was my first crack at the caper and if some of Marshall's flair for the dramatic could rub off on me I was still in with a chance of a top-12 finish. I pared the 16th and with two holes to play I was a shot out of the top 12.

I had to come up with something special on the par five 17th hole. "You've got to birdie or eagle this hole so let 'er rip," Dave told me as we walked to the 17th tee. I did just that and sent my tee shot way past Schneider's and Rosen's. They were virtually assured of top-six finishes even with pars or bogeys, so they played it safe. I was about 240 yards away from the pin. Dave handed me a three iron. I took my time, relaxed, and hit my best shot of the tournament. The ball landed on the green and rolled to within 12 feet of the pin.

"That was one heck of a shot," Schneider told me as we walked to the green. "Nail the putt and Deano and I will see you at Moonah Links."

Shit, like there isn't enough pressure on me, I thought as Dave handed me my putter.

After Schneider and Rosen each chipped onto the green it was showtime. I walked behind my ball, squatted like a baseball catcher, and examined the line. There was a slight break from left to right. Hit it too hard and the ball could roll right off the green. The putt needed the touch of a diamond cutter. About 200 people were on the fringe of the green looking on. I approached the ball, took a couple of practice strokes, and planted my feet. I took several looks at the hole just 12 feet away and backed away from the ball. "How the fuck do the pros on tour do this every week? My hands are shaking."

I took a couple of deep breaths and again approached the ball. I blocked everything else from my mind. It was just me, the putter, the ball, and the cup I struck the ball nicely and watched it roll to the left of the cup and then straight to it. My only worry was if it had enough pace. "Keep going, keep going. Don't come up short," I mouthed.

It didn't. It fell right into the cup with a revolution to spare for an eagle.

Five Iron and I exchanged high fives.

"Let's not get too carried away though. We still have one more to play," Dave warned.

I needed to par the 18th and last hole and did so.

"I think we've done it," Dave said as I scribbled a four on my scorecard. I looked at the leader board on the way to the scorer's hut. I was alone in ninth place with just three pairings left on the course. Baring a miracle by those behind me I had made it through the first round of Qualifying School. The only thing missing was some lovely running to me, throwing her arms around me and hugging and kissing me.

After emerging from the scorer's hut two reporters and a cameraman asked if I had a couple of minutes to spare. "You're on your own champ. I'll meet you in the clubhouse," Dave said. One reporter, Simon Turner, was from the local newspaper, the other and the cameraman from the Golf Victoria website.

They asked the usual questions; was it my first attempt at qualifying school? Did I think I had a chance the following week at Moonah Links?

"You seem to have come from nowhere," Turner said. "How did you ever get your handicap down by 20 shots in less than half a year?"

He had done his homework.

"I took long service leave from work – I'm a lawyer – and practiced and practiced and have a fantastic caddie who doubles as my coach," I answered.

Once they had their answers, I joined Dave in the clubhouse. He was nursing a cold one. We went over the official results. I had finished ninth, six shots behind the winner.

"I don't know if we can make up six shots in a week but at least we know the Moonah Links layout," I told Dave. "Those coming from Queensland, New South Wales and WA sections have probably never set foot on the course. And if the wind is blowing anything is possible."

We ordered another round of beers, then grabbed our gear, tossed it into the boot of my car and made our way back to the city.

At the top of the hour Dr Boyd Mendelsohn's receptionist, a woman even lovelier than her phone voice, called Marshall's name and told him to go to the first office on the left-hand side of a short hallway.

The door was open. Marshall knocked anyway. "Come on in Rich. It's a pleasure to meet you," he said as he came around from behind his large desk. The two shook hands and Mendelsohn motioned for Marshall to take a seat and get comfortable. Mendelsohn sat across from him and put a notepad and a pair of reading glasses on his lap. The room was nicely decorated. Two potted palm plants were in the corners closest to the door. A light breeze came through an open window behind Mendelsohn's desk.

"Have you ever seen a sports psychologist before?" he asked.

"I guess I've been pretty lucky. I haven't had the need to. I've never had a case of the yips or anything and I've been on the tour for nearly 30 years."

"You've had a pretty rough time since Augusta. How are you feeling? Do you think you're in a good place emotionally?"

"I won't lie doctor. It hasn't been easy. One day I'm a three-time Masters winner and the next I can't even hit a ball." He paused. "But Deidre and the kids have been great. They've offered me nothing but encouragement. Deidre was the one who suggested I see the doctors at the Mayo Clinic."

"You must be happy there is nothing physically wrong with you."

"I am. I was beginning to worry a bit."

"And how do you feel about being here today and rehashing everything? Because that is what we are going to do."

"I've gone over everything before with my swing coach, my caddie but we came up empty."

"How worried are you about not being able to get back to where you were?"

"On a scale of 1 to 10? Eleven. You're my last hope."

"Then let's get to it. Let's go back to that day at Augusta," Dr Mendelsohn said. "Did anything out of the ordinary happen that morning?"

"I went to the practice range like I always do to warm up. I hit 10 or 20 drives, hit a few balls with my irons and went to the putting green. I was hitting everything cleanly. I felt like I would have a really good tournament, at least finish in the Top 10."

"You were using your regular clubs? Nothing had changed since the last time you played?"

"Nothing."

"Anything happen at home with Deidre before you left?"

"Nothing. We ate breakfast together, had a few laughs. Then a car came and took me to the course, the same driver I've had for years. Deidre arrived later. I saw her in the crowd at the first tee."

"You met Riley Barnett, your playing partner, on the practice range?"

"Yes."

"Had you met Riley before?"

"No, but I had heard the name. Everyone on tour knows who the young up-and-comers are."

"Did you and he have a few cross words? An altercation of some sort?"

"Not that I can remember. He was very nervous as any kid would be preparing for his first round at Augusta. He was in awe of me a bit. He told me he had grown up watching me play on TV and that he was blown away to be practicing with me and to be drawn with Dusty (Johannson) and I."

"Then Riley and I walked back to the clubhouse. I met up with my caddie, he with his and we all walked to the first tee. Dusty joined us there and we waited for our names to be called by the starter."

Mendelsohn was scribbling notes into his pad but kept one eye on Marshall as he spoke.

"So, it was business as usual one would say."

"Yes."

Mendelsohn wrote in his notes that Marshall was relaxed and very forthcoming with his answers. His frustration though was evident.

"I just want an answer to what has happened to me. It's like someone flicked a switch and turned me into a hack."

Mendelsohn tried to put Marshall at ease.

"Close your eyes and think back to that Thursday. Block everything else out. You're at Augusta. You've come off the practice range."

Marshall closed his eyes and thought long and hard.

"Did you speak with anyone? Interact with anyone?"

There were always people shouting out his name, wishing him well. At least with the ban on cell phones inside Augusta he wasn't asked to pose for selfies. Off the course he didn't mind.

"Keep your eyes closed Rich and retrace your steps."

"There were two guys wandering around who seemed to be lost."

"They were fans?"

"I guess so. Nobody who works there, or any members of the press would ask for an autograph."

"And they asked you for an autograph?"

"One guy asked me to sign his hat."

"What sort of hat was it? Do you remember?"

"Yeah, one of the official Masters' hats with the insignia on the front."

"So, you signed it? "

"Yeah. They seemed nice enough."

"And then?"

"I think they wished me well."

"Anything else?"

"I'm trying to remember. I might have shaken the hand of the one who asked me to autograph his hat."

"There was no heckling involved of any sort?" Mendelsohn asked.

"No."

"And on your way to the first tee? Did you hear anything from a fan that might have gotten under your skin?"

"Not that I can remember. The fans do get after me sometimes for my gambling and the fact that I don't win as often as I should but it's all good-natured fun. I never take anything seriously."

Mendelsohn wrote down a few lines in his pad and then paused.

"Maybe on this day you did."

"And subconsciously it got to me?" Marshall asked.

"It's quite possible. If we can find out what was said and why it has affected your game, there's a chance we can get to the bottom of it and get you back on the course." But, Mendelsohn warned, "it is not going to happen overnight."

Marshall nodded.

"How were you sleeping prior to The Masters?"

"Alright I guess."

"Did you have any dreams in the weeks leading up to the tournament that were upsetting?"

"Not that I know of. Deidre would have told me if I was tossing and turning or talking or screaming in my sleep."

"It doesn't have to involve screaming Rich. Something which we brush off as minor can get into our subconscious minds and affect us when we're awake."

"You think that ...?" Marshall did not finish his thought.

"It's quite possible. Starting tonight," Mendelsohn continued, "I'd like you to keep a pad and a pen by your bed. If you are woken by a dream, write it down. And when you wake in the morning write down any dreams you can remember."

Marshall said he'd do it.

"Have you cured anyone of the yips, Doctor?"

"Several. For some reason golfers seem to respond better to treatment than let's say baseball players. I've worked with a couple of pitchers who suddenly can't throw a strike. There was a AAA outfielder a few years back, a good prospect mind you, who developed so many superstitions he eventually couldn't even get from the on-deck circle to the batter's box. They are part of a team Rich. They may feel like they are not only letting themselves down but their teammates and fans. With golfers it is just you against the course. Master the course and you master your opponents."

Marshall leaned forward in his chair. "That AAA outfielder you mentioned, it wasn't Robbie Brogan was it?"

Brogan was just 22, a high draft choice of the Los Angeles Dodgers. He was destined for stardom until he fell apart emotionally.

"No, it wasn't," Mendelsohn said. "But I wouldn't be able to tell you even if it was."

"I understand."

Mendelsohn closed his pad and took off his reading glasses.

"I'd like to see you again early next week if that is okay with you."

"That's fine. The sooner we get to the bottom of this – if we can – the better."

"Are you practicing at all?"

"I haven't touched my clubs in a week."

As he rose from his chair Mendelsohn told Marshall to get back to his usual routine.

"Before the Masters you hit balls every day?"

"Just about."

"I've read that you have nets set up at home. Is that true?"

"It is."

"When you get home hit a bucket of balls and do it every day. The sooner you get back into your usual routine the better you'll feel."

"Even if I'm hitting them like shit?"

"Yes."

The two shared a laugh and shook hands. Mendelsohn showed The Masters winner out, sat down at his desk and looked over his notes. "Fascinating case," he said.

Marshall made an appointment with the receptionist to see Dr Mendelsohn at the same time the following week. He stepped out of the office building, put on his sunnies to shield his eyes from the blazing desert sun and drove home. Feeling positive for the first time in weeks, Marshall went straight to the backyard and picked up a club. He did a few stretches, took a few practice swings, teed up a ball, pulled back his driver and watched his shot skid off the grass into the netting. "Shit," he screamed. He felt like breaking the club over his knee but instead stepped away from the tee, took a deep breath and scooped another ball from the bucket beside him. He kept swinging away, slicing, and hooking his shots, until he finally hit a decent shot. It was not the shot of a Masters winner, or even a pro, but it gave him a glimmer of hope.

I haven't played at Moonah Links in years and on the Monday before the final stage of qualifying school I head down to the peninsula to get reacquainted with the Moonah Links championship course. Two of the first four holes are over 500m long. Many of the par four holes are so dotted with bunkers you could be playing on the moon. If the wind kicks up – as it usually does on the peninsula – many of us will be lucky to break par.

Dave had to go back to work so I am on my own. I see a few of the others from stage one of qualifying school in the clubhouse and four of us – one of them being Reggie Cook, the 44-year-old accountant – decide to tackle the front nine. Cook birdied the 18th at Sandhurst to finally advance to the final stage of Q school.

"Think you've got enough magic left in those clubs of yours?" he jokingly asks as we walk to the first tee.

The cheeky remark takes me by surprise. "I sure hope so. This is one tough course, don't you think?"

"It's not going to be easy, that's for sure. I'd be very happy to shoot par."

"That's my aim too. Anyone who breaks par at this course deserves a tour card."

Cook later tells me he is juggling work and golf, often working late into the night to keep his job at a large accounting firm.

"You're on long service leave, aren't you?" he asks.

"I am. I've been on a course or driving range every day for the last few months and if I don't get my card this weekend I'll be back at work in January."

The four-day tournament begins on Wednesday. Those who finish in the top five when it is all over on Saturday gain automatic entry into 2019 PGA Tour of Australasia state championships and most Tier 1 tournaments on the pro tour in Australia. Those placing from sixth to 40th gain entry to most of the same events depending on their ranking.

I reckon there's no way I'm going to finish in the top 10. I've got a shot at placing in the top 20 if everything goes my way and some of the bigger names falter. Right off the bat I get a break with a lucky tee time of 8:15am on day one. I should be off the course by the time the wind kicks up in the afternoon.

Dave takes another three days off work to caddie for me and I shoot a one over 37 on the front nine and need to birdie the par five 18th to finish at par on the day. I somehow avoided the many bunkers on the 18th and am on the green in three shots, 15 feet from the hole. With the early leaders at four under, I desperately need to hole the putt. Dave warns me to use a very deft touch.

"If you hit it too hard you could easily roll right off the green." I take his advice and sink the putt for a massive birdie which gives me a huge shot of confidence. Dave and I want to jump up and high-five each other but the look we give each other is one that says, "save it for Saturday."

We're staying at the course's resort in a one-bedroom suite which is costing me $1000 for four nights. It will be money well spent if I get the tour card.

Dave and I plan our attack for day two which finds me five shots behind the leader. "We've got to birdie a few of those par fours if we're going to break par," Dave says over dinner. I concur and work on my iron shots on the practice range in the morning. We have an early afternoon tee time and the wind starts to blow right on schedule but not as fiercely as had been predicted. I start on the back nine and again shoot one under. I nearly came to grief on the par five fourth hole when I landed in a bunker but somehow got out of trouble and pared the hole. I birdied the par four sixth hole and shoot one under on the front nine and a 70 on the day. I'm two under after two days and in the top 20.

Showers arrive as predicted for Friday's third round and they prove to be more of a nuisance than a hindrance. I don't even bother putting on my rain gear. I huddle under the large umbrella Dave holds between shots.

About 50 kilometres away at Moorabbin Airport, 57-year-old Craig Harris is doing a safety check on his four-seat, single-engine Cessna 172 Skyhawk. He's filed his flight plan which will take him out over the peninsula to Queenscliff, and back towards Phillip Island before returning to Moorabbin.

It's a trial run for a sightseeing trip the next afternoon for three long-time bank employees who are being rewarded for their shifty and very profitable behaviour with a round of golf and lunch at Royal Melbourne, and the sightseeing trip.

Harris, a pilot for more than 30 years, has not flown for three months due to a back injury which needed surgery. "It feels good to be back aboard," he tells the radio tower before taxiing to the runway. It is 12:15pm. Skies are partly cloudy and the wind light. "Flight 274, you're clear for take-off," came through his earphones. "Have a good flight Craig."

Harris's Cessna took off and banked southwest towards the peninsula. It quickly gained altitude and several minutes later Harris levelled off at 8000 feet. The calm waters of Port Phillip Bay were on his right.

I was on the fairway of the par five fourth hole about to hit a five iron when I heard the sound of a single-engine aircraft. Dave and I each looked up. It's flying much too low. "Mayday, mayday. Flight 274, my engine's quitting on me. I'm going down," Harris barks into his radio. Looking to avoid any densely populated areas, Harris looks to his left and spots the wide-open spaces of Moonah Links Golf Course. He's about 300 feet above the ground and battling to control the aircraft. He activates the landing gear and spots a good area to put the plane down; the wide fairway of the long par five fourth hole.

The plane landed not even 50 feet from where Dave and I were standing. It bounced once and skidded into one of the bunkers bordering the green nose first where it burst into flames. The three players on the green at the time dove into one of the bunkers when they saw the plane coming their way. Dave and I ran to the plane and through the smoke saw the pilot struggling to get out. The heat of the fire pushed us back, but we managed to grab the door of the cockpit, yank it open and drag the pilot out. His pants and shoes were on fire, and we threw sand from the bunker on them to put out the flames.

About 10 seconds later the plane exploded. It sent debris high in the air which rained down on us. It missed us and the golfers huddled in the other bunker.

Dave took out his cell phone and called triple 000. Before his call was answered we heard sirens coming our way. I checked the pilot. His didn't appear to have broken any bones. He had a large cut on his forehead but was conscious. "My leg, my leg," he moaned. "Help is coming mate. Hang on," I told him. I almost lost my breakfast when I saw his burned right leg and I nearly fainted when I saw my right hand. My golf glove had melted from the heat of the door and was now part of my hand. The pain then hit me. I screamed louder than the sirens which approached. "What's wrong mate?" Dave asked. "My hand. It's fucked," I told him.

The emergency crews treated the pilot first, stabilised him and took him to the nearest hospital. They wrapped my hand, which by now was numb, in ointment and gauze and gave me some pain relief while fire crews put out the blaze.

Play was called off for the rest of the day and the remaining two plus rounds of the tournament were held on Moonah Links' Legends course. It's not as long at the championship course and easier to play.

The crash and rescue of the pilot was the lead story on the news on all three Melbourne-based TV channels that night. Footage from several golfers' mobile phones captured all the drama. The next morning's papers were filled with photos and stories on the crash.

Dave and I were hailed as heroes for pulling Harris out of the wreckage before it exploded. Thanks to our quick dousing of the flames on Harris's feet, his burns were not as severe as mine. Second degree the papers said. Harris also suffered a broken back in the crash and was never able to fly again. None of the doctors treating me for the third and fourth degree burns on my hand mentioned anything about returning to golf, but I knew my new career was over before it had even gotten started. I was forced to undergo a series of painful skin grafts and had to wear a glove on my raw right hand for months. The worst affected area was my thumb where the nerve endings were destroyed. It took ages to heal. It was hard enough to get a firm grip on a fork let alone a golf club.

I returned to work at Donaldson, Chafee and Howe in late January, nearly three months to the day I took my long service leave. The partners immediately put me on a team working on a class action lawsuit initiated by two dozen disgruntled superannuation customers of one of the big four banks. The case and trial went on for months due to the bank's constant stalling. The work took my mind off my injured hand which slowly improved thanks to the amazing work of the doctors, nurses and physios who looked after me. My private health insurance covered most of the cost. My out-of-pocket expenses were covered by the partners who netted a sizeable chunk of the nearly $40 million settlement awarded to our clients.

I occasionally caught up with Dave, Dom Williams and Ryan "Bubba" Watson for a few cold ones after work. I walked the course with them one Saturday morning when they played at Woodlands in Mordialloc but after that I stayed away from the golf course. It was too much for me to handle.

The Masters was held the first week of April and I turned on the TV on Friday morning to catch some of the opening round before I left for the office. Seeing the course again sent me back to Augusta where just 12 months earlier Dave and I watched Australia's own Jason Day win his first green jacket by sinking a 25-foot putt on the 18th green to avoid a play-off.

As I got dressed and finished my second cup of coffee, I heard the familiar voice of the starter stationed at the first tee. "Ladies and gentlemen, from Scottsdale, Arizona please welcome Rich Marshall." The applause was as loud as what Day heard last year on the 18th green.

Marshall doffed his baseball cap and waved to the crowd. I dropped everything and moved closer to the screen. Marshall waited until the applause died down before he placed his ball on the tee. He planted his feet and took a few practice swings. The crowd was silent. He brought his club back and struck the ball truly. It soared high into the air and landed some 300 yards away right in the middle of the fairway. The crowd roared as he walked off the tee and handed his driver to his caddie, Dr Boyd Mendelsohn. Each had a smile a mile wide.

In the Unlikely Event

t's a phrase heard by every passenger before the start of his or her journey – be it by plane, ship, train, bus, horse, or camel.

It's always made by someone in authority – the head flight attendant, the ship's captain, a train conductor, a bus driver. It can even be heard at a sporting event, the zoo or at the opening of a new building. For the most part it is widely ignored.

"In the unlikely event".

In the unlikely event the aircraft is forced to make an emergency water landing, the ship starts to sink, the train derails, the bus veers off the road, lions escape from their enclosure, the building begins to wobble from side to side; the message is quite similar: adopt the brace or crash position or muster if you're on a ship – and start filming your impending demise with your smart phone while holding it horizontally.

In the unlikely event; four words that could also be used for other rare occurrences.

For instance, in the unlikely event that North Melbourne wins a game in 2024 ... or ... the steering wheel becomes detached from the steering column.

Or ...

In the unlikely event Tiger Woods is your Uber driver.

In the unlikely event you land a job with your journalism degree.

In the unlikely event you sit through an entire episode of The Bachelor.

In the unlikely event your wife says yes to a threesome.

In the unlikely event the third person is your wife's twin sister.

In the unlikely event your car is serviced within an hour.

In the unlikely event you do not wake up from the anaesthetic.

In the unlikely event removalists show up on time.

In the unlikely event you are alive in the last leg of the quaddie and have half the field.

In the unlikely event a woman asks YOU out on Valentine's Day.

In the unlikely event your wife gives you a free pass on your 50th birthday.

In the unlikely event Donald Trump is elected president (It happened? Uh oh).

In the unlikely event Trump and Melania are seen holding hands.

In the unlikely event the head of the National Rifle Association is mortally wounded by his wife, who mistakes him for an intruder.

In the unlikely event you walk out of a dentist's office without spending more than $500.

In the unlikely event kids give YOU candy when you open your front door on Halloween.

In the unlikely event your proctologist did not wash his hands after examining his last patient.

In the unlikely event John Grisham does not have a new book out this Christmas.

In the unlikely event you cannot find a book by Bryce Courtney at your local op shop.

In the unlikely event you are asked what Hanukkah means and when it starts.

In the unlikely event a cop lets you off with a warning.

In the unlikely event the speed camera that clocked you doing 80 in a 60 zone is correct.

In the unlikely event Bill Shorten becomes prime minister.

In the unlikely event the hitchhiker you pick up is normal.

In the unlikely event your internet date looks she did in the photo she sent you.

In the unlikely event your NBN connection is as fast as promised.

In the unlikely event AFL or NRL grand final tickets find their way into the hands of the general public.

In the unlikely event your $10 pizza tastes good.

In the unlikely event you're able to find a rental in Sydney and Melbourne for less than $500 a week.

In the unlikely event a highly paid AFL player gives back half his salary because he had in his words "an off year".

In the unlikely event an AFL player kicks a goal from 20 metres out directly in front of goal.

In the unlikely event that someone from Mexico wins the pole vault at the next Summer Olympics (Trump's wall).

In the unlikely event your bus driver does not drive off after spotting you running towards the bus in his side mirror.

In the unlikely event Ben Simmons plays a full season without getting injured.

In the unlikely event the horse you are part owner in wins a race in town.

In the unlikely event your financial advisor is not a crook.

In the unlikely event more than 10,000 fans turn up for a Melbourne City soccer game.

In the unlikely event you laugh during an episode of "Tonightly with Tom Ballard".

In the unlikely event you are not seen leaving an adult shop by someone you know.

In the unlikely event you find a car park within an hour in the week before Christmas at Southland Shopping Centre.

In the unlikely event your electricity bill goes down.

In the unlikely event Hollywood makes a film that is not based on a comic book.

In the unlikely event you get a pay raise of more than two percent this year.

In the unlikely event this column appears in print or in a book.

The Cream Bun

J ust 20 minutes ago the sun was shining and there was barely a cloud in sight. But now the rain was pelting down so hard, I could barely see a car length in front of me. The only sensible thing was to pull off to the side of the road until the storm passed. Other cars kept whizzing by. "Schmucks," I yelled as they sped past and threw sheets of water up against the driver's side of my Toyota.

"Why am I even out in this kind of weather?" I asked myself. "I should be home watching Game 6 of the NBA Finals."

The text message arrived early in the third quarter. The Warriors trailed Toronto by a bucket and needed to win to force a seventh and deciding game back in Toronto, yes Toronto, that hotbed of basketball. Boston, Los Angeles, Chicago; that's where championships are won and lost. Not Toronto. Game six promised a heck of a finish. Even with all their injuries, I had a tenner on the Warriors at $1.90 and the over.

"I need a favour mate," the text read. "I need you to go to Hennessy's bakery in town, pick up a cream bun and deliver it to an office for me. It's very important. I can't do it. I'm in Launceston today."

Now ordinarily I would have replied ... ARE YOU FUCKING KIDDING ME? A CREAM BUN? But you see, the fellow who was asking the favour had helped me out of a financial jam just a week ago.

I had a five-leg multi going at the TAB and was all set to win a bundle until Carlton fucked it up and actually won a game. My $20 bet would have returned over $1400 and paid for my rent. The only thing I had in my pockets until my next pay day in a week's time was lint until Lenny Anderson bailed me out. "Pay me back when you can," he told me as he stuffed a wad of $50 notes in my hand.

So, feeling as if I had to return the favour, I headed to the bakery to pick up a cream bun. It started bucketing down two minutes after I pulled out of my driveway. I waited on the side of the road for 15 minutes. The storm passed just as quickly as it came and left a bright rainbow over the Mersey River. Just as I pulled into the shopping complex where Hennessy's was located, my phone beeped. "If that's a text from Lenny telling me he has changed his mind I'll buy a metre-long French stick and shove it up his arse," I hollered.

The text WAS from Lenny. Wanting to make sure his prized cream bun wasn't sold to someone else, Lenny told me he had called the bakery and asked them to put one aside for me. "When you get there tell them you want Jeff's cream bun," Lenny said.

I approached the counter and patiently waited until it was my turn to order. "Hi. A cream bun has been put away for me to pick up and pay for. Jeff's cream bun," I told the middle-aged woman behind the counter. She reached under the counter and pulled put a plain brown paper bag containing the cream bun. "That's $2.20," she said. I paid her and walked two blocks to a house which served as an accountant's office. I was supposed to ask for Denise, hand her the bag with the cream bun and say it was from Lenny. I made sure I had an umbrella with me in case the rain started up again.

The house was easy enough to find. I walked down the short front path to the front door and was greeted by a sign which read. "Please do not knock on the door. All our staff members are with clients. To speak with someone ring one of the numbers below."

You have got to be kidding, I said to myself. *What the fuck am I supposed to do with this cream bun?*

I knocked on the window. The sign said not to knock on the door but said nothing about the window. I waited and waited. "How long am I supposed to stand here?" I said out loud after five minutes. "I can't just leave it here."

I rang Lenny. The call went straight to his voice mail. "Ring the office and tell whoever answers that there is someone at the front door with a delivery," I said. I sent a text with the same message and waited. By this time the bun's cream had begun to stain the brown paper bag holding it.

Five minutes later a woman came to the door and opened it. Not all the way, but just enough to poke her head out to see who it was. "Are you Denise?" I asked.

In a soft voice she said, "I am."

"My name is Jeff Flanagan. I'm supposed to give you this. It's from Hennessy's and it's from Lenny."

Denise was a good sort; tall, slim with tight-fitting pants and about my age – mid to late 40s. She had a pretty enough face which was framed by light brown hair. *If Lenny is sweet on her, he's chosen wisely*, I thought.

With a puzzled and slightly bewildered look on her face, she gently took the bag from my hands, said thank you and closed the door.

I sent Lenny a text message. "Delivered. Denise is a cutie."

"Thanks pal," was his reply.

Later, after I finished watching the Warriors and my $10 go down the gurgler, I got a call from Lenny.

"Are you sweet on her?" I asked.

"Nah. It's a long story. I'll fill you in tomorrow over lunch. I'll be in town for the day.

"Working at the office with Denise?"

"That's the one."

Then why didn't you just get a bun in the morning and hand it to her in person I wanted to say. And ... I would have added. Take it from someone who has been married and been in several relationships. When a woman is handed a gift – no matter how small – by a third party (me) she will see that as a sign that you are interested in her.

"You see," Lenny told me over lunch the next afternoon. "I took her cream bun last Friday by accident. It was so funny."

Funny? I wanted to say. I've seen funny. I know funny. I'm a fucking comedian. And that is NOT funny. Embarrassing? Maybe. Awkward? A bit. But funny? No.

"Why don't you fancy Denise?" I asked. "I didn't see a ring on her finger. Does she like you?"

"She does. But she's not my type."

"Not your type? She's pretty, slim, fit, employed. What's not to like?"

Lenny took a bite out of a sandwich, put it down and looked straight at me. For a second, I thought my mouth was covered by the tomato sauce I was dipping my chips into.

"She's got big kneecaps."

"Big what?"

"Kneecaps. I've seen her in a skirt. Her kneecaps are all out of proportion."

"You're fucking kidding me, right?"

"No, I'm not."

"You're knocking someone back, someone who likes you, because her fucking kneecaps are too big?"

"Yes."

"You know, I thought I had heard every reason in the book for not liking a woman – and a lot of those reasons came from you."

I took a small notebook from my jacket pocket and began to read.

"She drinks too much, she smokes, she's a leftie, she doesn't like the footy, she's too short, too tall, her tits aren't big enough, her ass isn't small enough, I don't like her voice, her car, she doesn't floss, she can't cook, I don't like how she dresses, she snores, she's got a shit TV, her nails are too long, she goes to bed too early, she gets up too late, she won't have a bet on the Melbourne Cup, she slurps her soup, she's arrogant, she's pretentious, her ex is in jail, her ex just got released from jail, I don't like her glasses, she wears granny panties, she sleeps with a light on, her closet is a mess, she's a hoarder, she farts, she has bad breath, she's missing a toe on her left foot, she has a loud laugh, her taste in music is awful, she likes Vanilla Coke, she drives too slow, she drives too fast, she doesn't indicate, it's always that time of the month, she likes *The Voice*." On that I agreed.

"The book had been printed and the template thrown away," I told Lenny. "But now, we'll have to reprint the fucker to include big kneecaps."

Lenny shrugged. I put the notebook back in my pocket. He looked at the handful of chips left on my plate. "You going to finish those?" he asked.

"Help yourself mate."

I got up and put on my coat.

"Where are you going pal?" he asked.

"Back to that office to ask Denise out."

After Work **Drinks**

I t's Friday afternoon and Norm Graham is as nervous as a first-gamer having a shot at goal after the siren. He's got sweat stains under the arms of his light blue shirt and is perspiring despite the cool air pumping throughout the offices of Sanderson and Rosenstein, one of Melbourne's top advertising firms.

Graham is one of the firm's creative directors and he and his team have been working all week on a TV campaign for some new energy drink run by a couple of hipster doofusses, who are younger than he is. The story boards are supposed to be handed in by 3:30pm, just 75 minutes away. If he and Doug Faukner, one of the firm's other creative directors, like what they see they'll give the green light for a full-scale presentation to the bearded hipsters the following Wednesday. A lot is riding on the account but that's not why Norm Graham is so frazzled.

It's less than three hours before he meets a woman who works in the same building for an after-work drink. Sanderson and Rosenstein's offices are on the ninth floor. All he knows about her is that she works on the 12th floor for a law firm and doesn't have a wedding or engagement ring on her finger.

With his wavy brown hair and strong shoulders Norm is not a bad looking bloke. He turned 35 a few weeks ago and keeps himself fit. But he's missing the sleeve of tattoos and requisite beard which women in the 25 to

35-year-old age group seem to go for. He tried growing a beard a few years ago when the craze took off but his face and neck itched so much he went back to his regular shaving schedule of Monday, Wednesday and Friday.

Four times in the last two weeks Norm found himself in the same elevator with Jacqui Richards. He guessed she was about 30: give a take a year or two. It was just before nine in the morning each time. She carried a briefcase in one hand and a coffee in the other and was so immaculately dressed she looked like she had just walked out of a catalogue for an upscale boutique. A glittering chandelier hung from each ear.

She nodded when he looked in her direction. He said good morning on each occasion but was so intimidated by her good looks he couldn't get another word to come out of his mouth.

But yesterday morning he found himself alone in the same elevator with her for the first time. He kept waiting for someone to make a mad dash for the door before it closed but no one did. It was just the two of them now. He had less than 20 seconds to say something before the elevator stopped on his floor. Again, he said good morning. But this time added "on a sunny, warm day like this work should be cancelled."

Should be cancelled? Did I really say that? She's going to think I'm a moron, he thought.

But to his surprise she said. "I agree. It's too nice to spend a day like this inside."

He smiled, took a deep breath and extended his hand. "Hi. I'm Norm. Norm Graham."

She put her briefcase down, shook his hand and said "nice to meet you Norm, I'm Jacqui Richards."

Her hand felt warm in his. Just as their hands parted the elevator stopped on the ninth floor.

Norm turned to her as the door opened. It was now or never and to his surprise the words came out as smooth as lyrics from Tony Bennett's mouth. "Would you like to have a drink with me after work tomorrow Jacqui?"

As he said the word Jacqui, the elevator door started to close. He put his shoulder in front of it to give her a chance to answer. "Sure, that would be fun."

"How about Hennessy's? The one downstairs? Five okay with you?"

"Five it is."

Norm stepped out of the elevator. "See you then," he said.

Norm came in 45 minutes early on Friday morning to make sure he would be finished by five. A meeting with the owners of an upscale pet food company at 11 went better than he had thought. The husband-and-wife team were impressed with his presentation but said they wanted to sleep on it before committing. Norm would be in line for a bonus once they officially signed on.

Three floors above Jacqui Richards was getting a bit nervous as the clock on her office wall ticked closer to 5pm. *I hope we have something to talk about,* she wondered. *The last thing I want to talk about is work.* That was one of the reasons she politely declined the offers which came her way from her male co-workers.

She spent the afternoon crafting a strongly worded letter for a client who was suing one of the big four banks for negligence. Known for her toughness as a litigator, Jacqui was fairly confident the bank's lawyers would play ball before the case wound up in court.

At 4:45 she grabbed her handbag. Having decided to leave her briefcase in her office, she locked the door and went to the ladies room to freshen up before making her way to Hennessy's.

Hennessy's was beginning to fill up and it took a few minutes for Jacqui to get the attention of a bartender. She ordered a glass of white wine and took a seat at a table which faced the front door.

Norm was running late. He didn't get a look at the storyboards for the energy drink until a few minutes before four and it took more than an hour of sometimes heated discussion between him, Doug Faukner and the artists to agree on some minor changes before they were able to give the artwork the all clear.

Norm checked his watch. It was 5:05. "If you'll excuse me fellas, I've got to run. See you on Monday." He threw on his sports coat and sprinted to the elevator. He pressed the down button, removed his tie and shoved it in his jacket pocket, opened the top button on his shirt and waited, and waited some more. Finally, the elevator came. There was one guy in it. "Sorry mate, I'm going up to the 16th floor. Forgot my damn phone."

Norm stepped out of the elevator and again pressed the down button. It was 5:09. He thought for a moment about charging down the stairs but decided the sweaty and out-of-breath look would not be a good one.

At 5:15 he arrived at Hennessy's. He first looked for Jacqui at the bar and then noticed her sitting at a table meant to seat four. "Sorry I'm so late," he said as he sat down across from her.

"I had a meeting which went much longer than I thought."

"For a moment I thought you were going to stand me up," she jokingly said.

"Not a chance. Although I am going to stand up now and get a beer from the bar. Be right back."

Norm received a bit of a surprise when he returned. A casually dressed guy was sitting in the chair he had vacated less than three minutes ago and was chatting Jacqui up.

Puzzled, Norm looked at Jacqui.

"A friend of yours?" he asked.

She shook her head.

"I didn't know she was with you," the guy said apologetically as he got up. He was shorter than Norm was and backed away from the table with his hands up. "I don't want any trouble." He then turned and made a dash for the door.

"My hero," Jacqui said, fawning like a B Grade actress who had been rescued from the clutches of a mad villain.

Norm placed his beer on the table and sat down.

"Well, that's a new one. He ran off like I was going to pummel him."

"You ever been in a fight?"

"Not since I was about 10."

"Good. I'm not a fan of violence."

"Then I guess you wouldn't want to go to the Horn-Frazier fight with me tonight. I've got an extra ticket."

"Who?"

"Just kidding."

Jacqui smiled and took a sip of wine. "I like a man with a sense of humour."

"Well as soon as he gets here, I'll introduce you to him."

"Nah," Jacqui answered. "You'll do. But first ..."

Here we go Norm thought. This is where it all falls apart.

"Tell me about yourself. All I know about you is that you work in advertising."

"Okay, I've been with Sanderson and Rosenstein for the last six years. I'm one of three creative directors. We do TV commercials, print ads. I live about 10 minutes from here by tram. I follow Carlton in the footy, play a bit of golf occasionally, and don't mind seeing a good film if I can find one."

"And you?"

"I'm a lawyer. Taking on the top end of town gives me almost as much pleasure as watching Carlton lose."

"Why is that?"

"Cause I barrack for Collingwood."

Norm laughed. His beer was nearly finished. Jacqui's glass was on the low side as well.

"Where's home?" Norm asked.

Originally Gippsland. My family's still down there. I live in South Yarra. Two stops on the train and I'm here."

Norm looked at his glass and then hers.

"Want another? My shout."

"I'm afraid not. I've got plans. Maybe another time, okay?"

"Sure," Norm said. He felt like a hot air balloon which had sprung a sudden leak and was plummeting towards the ground.

Jacqui gathered her handbag, stood up, gave Norm a peck on the cheek and just like that was gone.

What the heck just happened? Norm asked himself. *Things were going so well.*

He replayed the conversation in his mind as he waited at the bar to get another beer. He couldn't think of anything that would have put her off. He took his beer and walked back to the table but it had been taken by four blokes, so he stood with his back against the bar and watched as dusk descended on Southbank.

As he did, he spotted Jacqui through the crowds. She was sitting on a bench near the footbridge to Flinders St Station. She had a cigarette in one hand and her phone in the other.

A moment later she was enthusiastically hugged by a bearded young bloke wearing skinny jeans. He thought the fellow looked like a Collingwood player, but he couldn't be sure. They shared a passionate kiss and took off arm in arm towards the station.

"Geez. You think you know someone," Norm said.

Chelsea

The ring of a cheap alarm clock woke Chelsea Wynwood at 5:20 on a cold and dark Tasmanian winter morning. She silenced the unwelcome noise by pressing the clock's snooze button, giving herself an extra five minutes of peace and warmth. When the alarm sounded a second time, she turned it off, peeled back her large doona and got out of bed.

Chelsea grimaced when her sock-covered feet hit the cold floorboards. She put on her slippers, grabbed a well-worn robe from the back of a chair and tightly wrapped it around her. She checked her phone; it was two degrees in East Devonport and not much warmer inside the old weatherboard rental. She walked into the kitchen, turned on the fluorescent light, and flicked on the kettle. As she walked to the bathroom to take a hot shower, the 28-year-old single mum saw her breath in the icy air. "I wish this old house had double-glazed windows to keep some of the chill out," she said.

On the nights her three-year-old daughter stayed at her grandmother's house, Chelsea didn't leave the heat on. She was paying over $225 a month as it was on electric bills. But when Jasmine was home, she set the living area's split system heater/air conditioner to 19° and warmed up the toddler's room with a small electric heater before she was put to bed.

Two years earlier Chelsea's former boyfriend and Jasmine's father ran out on them. If he had kept paying child support, she would have been able to keep her head afloat without having to ask for outside help.

Zack Stanaway left his wife and young daughter early one June morning to take a mining job on the mainland. The plasterer/handyman put what few belongings he owned into his small ute, left a note promising to drop $125 a week into Chelsea's bank account, laid low for a couple of hours and was one of the first in line to board the *Spirit of Tasmania* which was due to set sail for Melbourne at 9am. He parked the ute on level 5, made sure his toolbox was securely locked and joined the throng of day travellers filling the chairs and couches on level 7, one of three levels open to passengers. Private cabins for the nearly 11-hour crossing were available, but Stanaway didn't have an extra hundred dollars to spend and made himself comfortable on one of the couches in the public area.

He made a note of where the seasickness bags were since he tended to get a bit queasy when the swell picked up. Today he was lucky. The Mersey River was a flat as a pane of glass and the forecast for the journey across Bass Strait was for light winds.

The ship docked at Station St Pier in Melbourne just after 6:30pm. With 500 or so vehicles leaving the *Spirit* and hitting Beaconsfield Parade near the end of peak hour, it took over an hour for Stanaway and the others trapped in the bumper-to-bumper traffic to reach the West Gate Bridge. The traffic began to thin when he hit Geelong. He stopped for the night at the first cheap motel he found. It would take four days, maybe five, to drive to Kalgoorlie where a mate he used to play Under 18s footy with had a job waiting for him. "I want people working for me I can trust," Bob Malone told him in a phone call four weeks ago. "You'll make double what you're making now. You in?"

Zack was not the sentimental type and had never been all that keen about being a dad and a husband at the age of 24. When Chelsea told him she was pregnant and expected him to do the right thing and marry her, he had no other choice. The icy cold stares from Chelsea's two beefy brothers and father, a part-time truck driver, at a family gathering to celebrate the big news, left no doubt as to what would happen to him if he didn't.

At first Zack did his part. But after 16 months of Jasmine's constant crying and the changing of hundreds of nappies he'd had enough. He was never in love with Chelsea but loved how she looked. Chelsea was a stunner with long legs, full breasts, perfect teeth and dark wavy hair.

"We were just having a good time," he told a close mate, who would have traded places with him in a second.

But Zack and Chelsea disagreed over every little thing, from what baby food to buy to how they furnished their home. His meagre earnings left Chelsea with no choice but to find a part-time job. But when Zack took off and his weekly deposits into her account dried up six months later, Chelsea had to suck in her pride and march into Centrelink and ask for help. With Jasmine asleep in her pram, Chelsea filled out numerous forms and set up a myGov account online. Eight weeks later she received her first single parent allowance payment. It arrived every two weeks and along with occasional help from her parents and the money her job brought in she was able to pay her bills and care for herself and Jasmine.

When the *Spirit of Tasmania* was on time on its overnight sail from Melbourne, it docked in East Devonport just after 5:45am. When the ship was either early or late, Chelsea received a text message from her company which had the contract to clean the ship. Today there was no message which meant she had to be at the dock by 6:00.

She walked the four blocks from her home to the pier. Even before the first passengers began to head to their cars and motor homes parked on the lower decks of the ship, she and the rest of the cleaners were on a ramp heading to level seven to begin cleaning the ship's bathrooms, public areas and cabins.

Wading through the crowd waiting to disembark was the part of the job she hated most. There was always the same announcement. "Please step away from the doors to allow the cleaners through," a man's voice said. Chelsea and the other 20 or 30 cleaners walked through the parted crowd in single file. Many had their heads down to avoid eye contact with the passengers. Chelsea was one of them. *I would just die if someone I know saw me like this,* she thought. Even with her hair pulled back, not a drop of make-up and wearing an old pair of jeans, a grey sweatshirt and runners, Chelsea was by far the best looking one of the group. Several were in their 40s and 50s and looked 10 and 20 years older. Cleaning sinks and toilets, stripping and making beds, and vacuuming was back-breaking work. It seemed that for every month you worked you aged two.

Today the seas were calm so there was hardly any puke to clean-up from sea-sick passengers.

Four hours later Chelsea and her team were finished with their shift. All the cleaning supplies and vacuum cleaners were packed away. Cabins were ready for the next batch of passengers who would board the ship later that afternoon for the night-time sail to Melbourne.

Chelsea's mum, a retired secretary for a builder in Devonport, planned to bring Jasmine by the house around noon giving her just over an hour to wind down. As she trudged home under sunny skies, the mobile in her bag pinged. It was a message from her best friend Violet asking if she wanted to have a coffee. Chelsea was dead tired but hadn't seen Violet in several weeks and agreed to meet her at a new cafe in East Devonport. It was a few minutes after 11 when Violet drove up in a bright red Mazda that didn't even have 10,000ks on it. Chelsea was already inside, sipping a hot coffee which gave her a bit of energy.

"Over here," Chelsea called out when Violet opened the front door.

Violet gave Chelsea a big hug, threw her handbag on the chair next to her and turned and asked a young woman standing behind a display case filled with muffins and cakes for a latte.

"You look beat Chelsea."

"I am. These early morning starts, and the cold weather are just sucking the life out of me Violet. If the money was better, it might not be so bad, but to tell you the truth I'm wondering if it's worth it. I'm scrubbing toilets for fuck's sake."

Violet gently rubbed her long-time friend's free hand. "I'm sorry to hear that hun. But it is worth it. Think of that wonderful little girl of yours while you're working. It will help."

"I do."

Violet Thompson wouldn't last a day if she had to scrub toilets for a living and she knew it. Her family was one of the few in town who were able to afford a modern waterfront home. They even had a woman come in to clean twice a week. Her father was part owner of the biggest trucking company in town. Chelsea's father drove one of those trucks to Launceston and back several times a day two or three times a week. Hank Wynwood wanted more hours, but his emphysema caused by over 50 years of smoking gave him coughing fits and had him tethered to an oxygen tank for days at a time.

Violet didn't have any money troubles of her own. She was engaged to some hot-shot salesman at one of the local car dealers and worked four days a week for the local council. This afternoon she would be working behind the main counter, issuing dog and cat licences and directing residents with questions or complaints to the proper department.

The two exchanged gossip on some mutual friends before Violet asked Chelsea if she had heard from Zack. "Not a peep," she answered. "I don't even know where the hell he is."

"I don't suppose he's gotten around to sending you any money."

"Not a cent."

Chelsea paused to polish off what was left of her coffee and continued. "Jazz is going to grow up not knowing who her father is and that's not going to be easy for her."

"No, it won't. But better not knowing who he is than knowing what an arsehole he is."

"You're right."

Violet checked her watch. "I better get going. If I'm not back by 11:45 I'll hear about it. "I'm glad we were able to catch up. If there's anything I can do let me know, okay?"

Violet kissed Chelsea on the cheek, grabbed her bag and went to the counter where she paid for her coffee and ordered a blueberry muffin. She held the muffin up for Chelsea to see. "Something for later," she said. She walked to her car parked out front and sped off.

Chelsea sat at the table for a moment and glanced at an old clock hanging on the wall to her left. She had 30 minutes to kill before her mum dropped Jazz off and decided to have another cup of coffee before she went home.

Sitting on the table next to her was a copy of the local paper. She took it and started to thumb through it from back to front the way she used to when her brothers were playing footy and cricket. On the page facing the obituaries, which she always checked to see if anyone she knew had passed away, were the classifieds which barely filled a page. A couple of cars and some farm equipment were for sale along with a small ad for a house for rent which had been there for nearly a month. "They're asking too much for it. Nobody here can afford $375 a week for rent," she said out loud. The cafe was all but empty, so no one heard her. There were ads for annual general meetings of a handful of cricket and footy clubs in the area but what caught her eye were the numerous ads under the heading of Adult Services. She counted them. There was 16 of them, 10 of them with photos of young Asian women – head shots only – promising good service (in or out) DD breasts, size four bodies and long dark hair. Each ad had a mobile number and the words *No Texts*. Some were in town for a week, others for only a night or two. Three ads touted the fact that pics were available. *I'd want to see pics too before meeting one of them*, Chelsea thought.

Just three of the ads were from women claiming to be Australian.

Is this really what guys want? she asked herself. *To screw a woman whose been with five or six other blokes the same day?* She wondered how much the women charged. Would have to be at least $200. Screw five a day and you walk away with $1000, in cash.

Chelsea did the numbers in her head. It took her a month to bring home $1000.

With just one other table occupied and the woman behind the counter serving someone through the takeaway window, Chelsea ripped the page with the ads out of the paper and stuffed it in her coat pocket. She tossed the paper back on the table she got it from, got her things together and walked home. Her mum and Jasmine were there waiting for her, parked behind her aging Holden in the carport.

"Sorry I'm late," she told her mum. "I stopped and had a coffee with Violet."

"That's okay," Catherine Wynwood said. "We just got here."

Jasmine's face lit up when she saw her mum. She kicked her feet as Chelsea got her out of her car seat while her mum grabbed an overnight bag from the front seat.

"Were you a good girl for grandma?" Chelsea playfully asked her daughter.

Jasmine nodded enthusiastically.

"She was a doll," Catherine Wynwood said. "She didn't play up once."

Chelsea turned the heat up to 19 as soon as the three walked in the door. A bit of sun peeking through the curtains helped warm up the living area. "I've got to get going. Your dad has a doctor's appointment in an hour," Catherine Wynwood said.

"Okay. Give Dad my best and thanks again for looking after her."

"My pleasure sweetheart. We love having her."

Catherine kissed her granddaughter goodbye, then her daughter and closed the front door behind her. They would do the whole thing again in two nights time when Chelsea had her next shift. She couldn't afford to pay a babysitter and didn't know anyone she could trust. Chelsea hung up her coat and took Jasmine's off. A red and green sweater, a Christmas gift from grandma, kept the three-year-old warm until the room heated up.

"What do you say we have some lunch Jazz? Peanut butter and jam?"

"And juice."

"Of course. One can't have a sandwich without juice."

Chelsea put her daughter in her highchair, turned on the TV and fed the movie *Finding Nemo* into the DVD player. Jasmine had seen it about 50 times but never got tired of seeing the cute clown fish and his pals.

Chelsea brought Jazz's sandwich to the table and watched her daughter bite into the soft white bread. "Good," she said. "Good."

When it was time for Jasmine's afternoon nap, Chelsea gently placed her tired daughter in her bed and covered her with a warm doona. She pulled the curtains together to block out the afternoon sun, kissed Jasmine on the forehead and left the door open.

Chelsea went to the coat rack by the front door, reached into a pocket and pulled out the page she had torn from the newspaper. She sat down on her couch and again looked over the ads, circling the one by an Asian woman which said couples were welcome. She decided to ring, rehearsed what she was going to say, reached for her phone and punched in the number. A woman answered after three rings.

"Hi," Chelsea nervously said. "I'm calling about your ad in the paper. You say couples are welcome?"

"Yes, very welcome," a young woman replied in nearly perfect English. "For you and your husband?" she asked.

"Yes. We're looking to spice things up a bit in the bedroom."

"I can do that," the child-like voice said. "I entertain a lot of couples."

"This entertaining ... ummm how much do you charge?"

"It all depends if I come to see you or you visit me."

"We would rather come and see you. We have very nosey neighbours."

"Tiffany" ran down the prices like she was working at a takeaway. An hour for the two of them would be $300. For just her husband $225. Payments were cash only. Her "office" was a motel in town. Tiffany was available from noon until late.

Chelsea wrote the figures down and said she would have to talk with her husband before making any appointment.

"That's okay hun. My afternoons are booked but I am free the next two nights. After that I go to Launceston."

Chelsea said she would ring back if her husband agreed.

"You won't regret it," Tiffany said. "My clients say I'm the best in the business. Just one thing, condoms are a must. I'll send you a photo so you can see what is waiting for you."

Chelsea thanked her and ended the call. She felt like a young kid who had just made a crank call.

Two minutes later a text message from Tiffany arrived with a photo. She was just as her ad said, if in fact the picture was her own. She had a youngish face with long dark hair and was wearing just a bra and panties and high heels. She couldn't have been more than 22 or 23. The large breasts were obviously fake, and Chelsea figured she wasn't more than a size six.

If I was a guy I would surely be tempted, she thought. She figured a guy would spend about $100 on dinner and drinks on a date. For another $125 he'd get laid and that would be the end of it. No small talk, no phone calls. She rarely thought of Zack but pegged him as someone who would sleep with one of these girls. No commitments, not a chance of her getting pregnant.

Chelsea spent the next hour or so wondering if she would be able to sleep with a stranger for money. *Could I do it here? In Devonport? What if I knew the guy? I'd be known as the Devonport whore. I'd have to go to a neighbouring town and have upscale clients.*

Chelsea went into her bedroom and looked at herself in the full-length mirror which hung on the back of the door. *I'm better looking than this Tiffany. I could do my hair, go all out with the make-up, wear a short skirt, heels; show off my boobs.*

She hadn't slept with anyone since Zack took off and did miss the sex. She had a battery-operated boyfriend in her underwear draw she used once or twice a week. But could she sleep with a stranger? Would she be safe? There were stories everywhere about hookers being beaten and, in some cases, murdered. But they mostly worked the streets in Melbourne and Sydney.

What if I call myself an escort? I've never heard of an escort being hurt. They're screwing politicians, businessmen, guys who wear suits. They have reputations to protect.

Chelsea took a sheet of A4 paper from her printer, found a pen and sat down at her kitchen table. *What would I put in an ad?* she wondered. As she started to write she heard Jasmine stir and then start to cry. She quickly walked into her daughter's bedroom and picked Jasmine up. "What is it sweetheart?" she asked. With one whiff of her diaper she knew.

After Jasmine had been put to bed for the night, Chelsea went back to working on her ad. It took four tries for her to get the wording right and even then, she wasn't sure if it was good enough to attract enough attention.

Tall, attractive, sexy Aussie gal, mid 20s, size 8, busty (real). You won't be disappointed. Fri, Sat only. No texts.

A mobile number from a cheap throwaway phone would follow. She wasn't about to put her mobile number or photo in the ad.

Chelsea looked at her work roster which was taped on the fridge. In two weeks she had both Friday and Saturday off. She could tell her mum she was working the afternoon and early morning shifts and ask if she could take Jasmine both days so she could get some much-needed sleep. If her mum pressed her on why she was working a double shift she'd say she needed the extra money to see the dentist. She decided to pay for the ad in cash at the newspaper's local office instead of by credit card to avoid using her name and have the ad appear only in the company's sister paper in Launceston. She did need a name though for the ad and for her clients and settled on Sarah Carrera. *It sounds exotic and erotic*, she thought.

Her idea was to drop Jasmine off at her mum's at noon on Friday and drive the hour to Launceston and get a room at the classy Country Club Resort. She'd stay for two nights – at $159 per – and return on Sunday morning. She was hoping for four clients each day. The $225 she charged each client would give her an even $1800. Her expenses were the room, petrol there and back, $50 for the ad, and a new mobile phone, nearly $500 in total. Not a bad profit for two nights work.

Two days later while her mum and dad were looking after Jasmine, Chelsea drove into town. She parked across the street from the newspaper's office, tucked her shoulder-length brown hair under a baseball cap, put on a pair of sunnies, reached into the backseat for a jacket she rarely wore and put her plan in motion. She went into Kmart and bought the cheapest mobile she could find and a SIM card. It set her back $69. She jotted the new number down and crossed the street to the newspaper's office.

She took a deep breath and opened the door.

"I'd like to place a classified ad please," she told a middle-aged woman at the front counter.

She was given a classified ad form attached to a clipboard and moved a couple of steps to her left to fill it out. At the top of the form were the names of two newspapers. She ticked the name of the Launceston paper and then a box for the ad to appear under the Adult Services heading. She neatly copied what she had written down at home. She checked the new number twice to make sure she had written it down correctly and handed the clipboard back.

"Are you sure you don't want the ad in the local paper. It would cost just another $10," she was asked. "No thank you. Just the Launceston paper please." She handed a $50 note across the counter, was given a dollar coin back, turned and walked to the door.

"Oh Miss," the woman called out.

Chelsea panicked. *Maybe she knows me*, she thought.

"You forgot to fill in the dates you want the ad to appear."

"I'm sorry, the Thursday through the Sunday, the week after next, the 20th to the 23rd. Thank you."

Chelsea walked out the door, took a deep breath, waited for the light to change and walked back to her car. She was sweating on a cool and overcast day. She took off her sunnies and baseball cap, let her hair down and reached for a bottle of water that was laying on the passenger seat. *I don't know if I can go through with this.*

For the next week Chelsea was as nervous as a cricketer walking to the creases for her first senior game. She didn't tell a soul about her plans and spent hours trying on different outfits. When she found the right one; a low-cut top, slit skirt and matching heels she packed it away in a small suitcase and left it in the back of her closet. Over the weekend she bought a box of condoms and a tube of lube and tossed both into the bag.

Several days later, with Jasmine tucked into her pram, Chelsea walked to the nearest newsagent. She always walked to the Spirit and to the local shops to keep in shape, even when the wind was up as it was today. She wheeled the pram inside and over to where the newspapers were displayed, picked up the Launceston paper and flicked to the classified pages. Her ad was third from the top, one of a dozen. Eight had photos of Asian women, the four other ads contained just words. She read her ad, then read it again. It was just as she had written down on the form. Her new phone could ring at any time, so she brought it with her just in case. It was just after 10am. She hoped it would not ring while Jasmine was with her. Better for it to ring when she was napping or at her grandma's. She needn't had worried. The phone didn't ring once all day. After Jasmine was put to sleep Chelsea rang the new mobile just to see if it was working. It was. She decided to leave a voice message and rehearsed it a few times before she recorded it. "Hi. You've reached Sarah. Leave your details and I'll ring back as soon as I can. Bye."

She rang the mobile to listen to the message and decided it wasn't sexy enough. She deleted the message, recorded another and played it back. Satisfied with it she put the phone down and turned on the TV. She had one eye on *The Bachelor* and the other on the phone. One hour ticked by, then two. She turned off the TV and spent the rest of the night flicking through the paper her ad was running in. The phone sat on the coffee table in front of her.

Shit. What if I don't get any responses? she thought. *It'll be nice to get away for a few days, but I'll be out $500. Damn. What was I thinking?*

Early the next afternoon she dropped Jasmine off at her parents' house. She gave her mum a bag with a few changes of clothes, a handful of DVDs, some cartons of juice and half a dozen tubes of strawberry yoghurt.

"I'll be pretty busy over the next couple of days Mum," she said picking up Jasmine. "Send me a few text messages to let me know how she's doing. I'll be grabbing some sleep whenever I can."

"I'll do that sweetheart," Catherine Wynwood promised.

"You be a good girl for grandma and grandpa, okay? I'll see you in a couple of days." Chelsea kissed her daughter goodbye and put her in Catherine's arms. "Say hi to Dad for me. I'll see him on Sunday," she said as she closed the front door.

An hour later Chelsea was on the road to Launceston. She placed her "work" mobile on the passenger seat. It had still not rung. She filled her reliable Holden at a petrol station on Bass Highway and fiddled with the radio before getting back on the road. Her car was so old, with over 200,000ks on it, that it didn't have a CD player. When an old Tom Jones song came on the radio, she flicked it off. The sound of cars and large trucks whizzing past, well over the 110kph speed limit, was better than *What's New Pussycat?*

Ten minutes later the sun made its first appearance of the day. The car warmed up quickly, so she cracked the window and took her jacket off while keeping one hand on the wheel. Just as she entered the perfectly manicured grounds of the Country Club Resort and passed the golf course, her "work" phone sprang to life. She pulled into the massive parking lot and picked it up before the call went to voicemail. "Hi. Sarah speaking."

After working the past two nights proofreading a manuscript by a right-wing, Trump loving, climate-change denier which needed two ghost writers to make it readable, Dennis Matthewson had been given the afternoon off. He felt like taking his eyeballs out of their sockets and rinsing them out before leaving the heritage-listed building which housed Tas Publishing, an accounting firm and a proctologist.

On his way out Matthewson was handed a gift certificate by Callum Woods, his boss of the last two years, for a round of golf at the Country Club Resort. "I really appreciate the work you did on this Dennis. Charlie Preston is an arsehole of the highest order. We all know that. I don't believe a word of what he says or writes but there's a market for his brand of crap and the money we make off it will allow us to publish half a dozen other books, real books, that otherwise would never see the light of day."

"Maybe we should give Preston's next manuscript to Dr Madison on the first floor. He'll find enough shit in it to keep him busy an entire day," Matthewson said.

Woods laughed. "See you on Monday," he said.

Matthewson walked outside and shielded his eyes from the bright sunshine. It was at least 10 degrees warmer than it had been three and a half hours earlier. His car was one of 10 parked in a small lot adjacent to the building that tenants had the use of. Tas Publishing had three spots, two of which went to Matthewson and Woods. The other was given out on a rotating basis. Those missing out were forced to park on the street two blocks away which was not ideal thanks to Launceston's fickle weather.

Matthewson checked his cheap watch. It was 12:40. He hadn't had an entire Friday afternoon off in the six years he worked for Tas Publishing. He took the gift certificate out of his shirt pocket and gave it a look. It was due to expire in three weeks. His clubs, golf buggy and shoes were in the boot. Ten minutes later he was in the parking lot of the Country Club Resort. He parked halfway between the golf course and the casino. The plan was to have lunch, have a look around, gather his gear and get at least nine holes in.

Matthewson washed down a burger and chips with a cold beer. He couldn't remember the last time he had a beer so early in the day. Matthewson was 42 years old and an average looking bloke at best. He played golf two or three times a month with a couple of mates who he had known for years and jogged occasionally to keep fit. He was unmarried, owned a two-bedroom unit in one of Launceston's better neighbourhoods and drove a three-year-old Mazda.

Except for the annual Tas Publishing Christmas party, Matthewson didn't socialise with his dozen colleagues. He preferred the company of books and newspapers. They didn't talk his ear off and bore him to tears. He did his reading in his unit's second bedroom which he turned into a study. The walls were lined with hundreds of books, many of which he received free from his friends at other publishing houses. Some were uncorrected proofs and desperately needed the deft hand of an experienced editor and an eagle-eyed proofreader. An old desk and a comfortable chair rounded out the decor. He watched the news most nights in the living room but apart from the footy on Friday and Saturday nights his television was off by 8pm unless he found something on Netflix which interested him. He ate dinner alone, usually something he picked up from an upscale market on the way home and hadn't had a woman in his unit since he and Marci Nelson parted company three and a half years ago. She wanted to get married and have children. Matthewson wasn't averse to the idea of marriage but the idea of being a dad scared the crap out of him.

"It's a never-ending job, you're on call 24-7 and I'm just not cut out for it, Marci," he told her one night after dinner. "I'd be a nervous wreck. I would much rather read a book in peace than have to listen to a screaming baby, change diapers and go to parent-teacher meetings."

"At least you're honest Dennis. You'd be such a good dad. You're going to miss out on so much."

"You may be right. But ..."

For once the man who made his living with words couldn't come up with the right ones, or any for that matter.

Marci Nelson put on her coat, grabbed her handbag, kissed Dennis on the cheek and walked out without saying another word.

Eight months later Matthewson found out from a mutual friend that Marci was engaged to a lawyer. He wasn't invited to the wedding but sent her a text message when she gave birth to a healthy baby boy 20 months after they parted ways. Marci never replied and only two months ago became a mum for the second time. "Two kids in less than three years? There's no way I would have been able to cope," Matthewson said.

Matthewson grabbed his clubs, buggy and shoes from the boot of his car, put a pair of sunnies on his nose, a baseball cap on his head and wheeled his clubs to the pro shop. The parking lot closest to the course was less than half full so he didn't think there would be much of a wait.

Matthewson handed his voucher to a young bloke behind the counter who he recognised from his photo which had recently appeared in the local paper. He had won an amateur tournament in a cakewalk over the best amateur golfers Tassie had and was fielding several offers from big clubs in Melbourne which wanted him to play pennant golf for them.

"There's two foursomes ahead of you," Glenn Schuester said. "The wait will be 20 minutes tops and if someone else comes along while you're waiting, I'll have to pair you up with him."

"Not a worry," Matthewson said.

He put on his golf shoes, which needed to be replaced, and made his way to the practice putting green. To his surprise, most of the putts, even the 20-footers, wound up in the bottom of the cup.

Twenty minutes later Matthewson heard his named called and marched to the first tee. No one else had shown up so it was just him and the course for the next few hours.

While his putting was as good as it was on the practice green, his drives were awful. He hit just two of the first eight fairways, lost two balls and was 16 over par after nine holes. It was just after 4pm. He looked up. Clouds were moving in and had obscured the sun. With the wind picking up, Matthewson decided to call it a day.

He put the covers back on his clubs, took off his golf shoes and walked to the near-empty clubhouse. He parked his buggy and went inside. A couple of dozen golfers were seated around a handful of tables. Matthewson ordered a beer at the bar and grabbed a seat away from the others. A copy of the local paper was laying on his table. He picked it up and turned to the sport section. He flicked through it, from back to front, and stopped at the racing page. There were 22 minutes until the next-to-last race at Bendigo. He checked the latest odds on his phone and was surprised to see a last-start winner trained by the Hayes boys at the price of $8.60. *I've got plenty of time to get over to the casino*, he thought.

He turned the page where the ads in the Adult Services section were displayed. Several were bathed in red ink and contained provocative photos. They were hard to avoid. Matthewson glanced at them. All but two were based in Launceston. Even without a photo, Chelsea's ad stuck out. Instead of just ripping Chelsea's ad from the paper, Matthewson went to the bar and asked for a pen.

"A pen? Don't you want another beer mate?"

"Nah. Just a pen. I'll bring it right back."

"It's alright. Keep it. We've got a million of the bloody things."

Matthewson wrote down her number on a serviette, grabbed his buggy and bag and jogged to his car. He stashed everything in the boot and checked his watch. He had six minutes to get a bet down on the race at Bendigo. Not being an everyday punter and a bit sceptical about online wagering, Matthewson made his bets in person.

He ran from the parking lot into the casino, got on the escalator and took two steps at a time. The UniTab wagering outlet was behind the pokie machines and table games. He checked the latest odds on the TV closest to the betting window. Brave Lad was still holding firm at $8.60. The 11 horses in the 1200m sprint were being led into the starting gate and thankfully there was no one waiting in line at the counter. Matthewson quickly filled out a betting card, marking $20 to win and $10 to place on the number 6 horse, Brave Lad. Five seconds after his betting card went through the machine the gates crashed back and the field took off.

Matthewson stood in front of one of the many large TVs and looked for Brave Lad's blue and white silks. His jockey settled him just behind the speed, peeled out of the pack with 300m to go and stormed home to win by a length. "Yes," he shouted. When the prices came up on the screen Matthewson did a bit of math. The $8.60 to win price and $3.00 place price gave him $202.00. He sat down to catch his breath and when correct weight was announced he collected his winnings.

There was a very short-priced favourite in the last at Bendigo which Matthewson wanted no part of. He got a glass of water at the bar and wiped a few beads of sweat from his brow with a serviette. *Five seconds later and I wouldn't have gotten the bet on. First, I get the afternoon off, then the free game of golf and now this. Are the gods on my side?* he wondered.

He was about to find out. With nothing to lose, Matthewson had a look at the table games. There were a couple of punters at the lone crap table in operation and a half dozen men were tossing chips on the roulette wheel's colourful felt table. Matthewson had never completely understood craps so he tossed two twenties on the roulette table and received $40 in chips. He glanced at the last five numbers which had come up; 21, 33, 9, 17 and 5; all odd numbers. He bet $30 on the next number being an even one and put a $5 chip on number 22, his golf handicap. The croupier spun the wheel and loudly announced "No more bets". He then released a small ball in the opposite direction the wheel was turning. The ball eventually lost its momentum and bounced several times before landing on number 22. Matthewson banged his fist on the railing in celebration. The dealer scooped up all the losing chips and paid Matthewson his winnings in chips. Thirty-six to one for his $5 wager on number 22 and even money on the $30 evens bet. He pocketed another $200 plus dollars in chips and walked away.

Being that it was 4:30 in the afternoon, there was only one blackjack table in operation. Not a single person was playing. The dealer stood motionless on the other side of the table like a guard at Buckingham Palace. Later that night every table would be in operation and every seat taken. On a Friday and Saturday night thousands of dollars exchanged hands every minute.

Matthewson hadn't played a hand of blackjack since he was in Melbourne more than five years ago. He lost $50 that night in a blink of an eye and swore he would never play a casino game again. But emboldened by his wins at the roulette wheel and the races, Matthewson sat down at the table and said hello to the dealer. The dealer nodded. He was a youngish looking fellow, no more than 25 or so and looked like a Park Avenue doorman in his casino garb. A nametag was attached to his vest. "Six decks Lance"? Matthewson asked.

"Yes, with a $10 minimum bet."

Win or lose Matthewson was only going to play one hand and walk away. He took eight $25 chips from his pocket and placed them on the table.

Lance dealt the cards from the shoe. He had a face card and a three showing. Matthewson peaked at his two cards which were face down. He had a jack and an eight. "I'm good," he said letting go of the cards.

The dealer took the next card out of the shoe and flipped it over. It was a nine. Twenty-two, a bust.

Matthewson let out a sigh of relief and clapped his hands. The dealer gave him eight more $25 chips. Matthewson stood up, put the chips in his pocket, thanked Lance and walked straight to the cashier's window. He slid all of his chips across the counter to a woman who carefully counted and stacked them. "Would you like large bills," she asked. "Yes please," Matthewson answered. She handed him four $100 bills. He stuffed the bills into his front left pocket turned and walked off. He ordered a Diet Coke at the bar, in case he decided to head home, took it to a nearby table and sat down. It was after five and the place was beginning to fill up. Using the pen he got from the clubhouse, he added up his winnings on the back of the serviette which had Chelsea's number. Just over $600 in half an hour. He hadn't had a day this good since the 2010 Melbourne Cup when he had the winner, Americain, the exacta and trifecta and pocketed over $1200.

He turned the serviette over and looked at Chelsea's number. He hadn't been with a woman in 18 months. Women just didn't go for him. He was a nice guy and all but was told by more than one woman he wasn't good looking enough. Shunned, Matthewson cranked one out a few times a week to make sure everything was still in good working order. He thought about Marci when he did. She was the exception. She didn't care about his looks or lack of them. She liked him for who he was, a decent, caring guy who made a good living, made her laugh and never once raised his voice in anger.

Should I ring this Sarah? he wondered. Since she was only going to be in Launceston for two days Matthewson figured she was from out of town. *There's no way she'll know who I am and I'm $600 richer than I was 30 minutes ago.*

He took a deep breath and rang the number. It rang and rang and was about to go to voicemail when Chelsea picked it up. "Hi, this is Sarah. Who's this?"

"Hi Sarah. My name is Dennis. I saw your ad in the local paper and am wondering if you are free tonight?"

"I am Dennis. What time would you like to come by? I have a room at the Country Club Resort."

"Do you really? I'm there now having a drink at the bar."

Chelsea liked the sound of his voice. "Small world isn't it?"

"Very. I was going to have dinner in a bit. I hear there's an excellent buffet here. Want to join me Sarah? My treat. Then we can talk about that appointment of ours."

Chelsea did some quick thinking. *It would be safer to meet him in a public area than have him just knock on my door and walk in. I was going to have dinner anyway. Why not. He's treating. If he's a jerk I'll tell him to forget about any appointment.* "Okay, can you give me about 30 minutes? I just got out of the shower."

"Sure, take your time. I'm in the bar on the second floor, the one near the TAB. I guess you'd call it the sports bar."

"How will I know you?"

"I'll have a dark sports jacket on and a bunch of winning tickets in my hand."

Chelsea laughed. "Want me to send you a photo so you know who I am?"

"No need," Matthewson said. "I'd like to be surprised."

You won't be disappointed, Chelsea thought. "Okay," she answered.

"It's a little after five now. Make it at 6."

"See you then Dennis. Bye."

She sure sounds nice, Matthewson thought as he put his phone back in his pocket.

Matthewson finished his soda. He needed to go back to his car and get his sport jacket. In the rush to get his racing bet on he had forgotten it. He slowly walked to the escalator and rode it to the main entrance downstairs. The resort was filling up. Some country music star Matthewson had never heard of was playing in the resort's showroom that night and the next. Cars were streaming into the parking lots. Matthewson found his Mazda. Utes were parked on either side of him. He saw several blokes put on their cowboy hats as they stepped out of their cars. He wished he had an extra shirt, a clean and fresh one, stashed in his car or golf bag. There was no time to go home and change so he put on his sport coat, locked the car and walked back inside. He went to the toilet and cleaned up the best he good. He splashed some water on his face, wiped his moist arm pits with wet paper towels and thoroughly washed his hands. He was presentable.

Matthewson rode the escalator back to the second floor, ordered another Diet Coke, found a free table and watched the harness and greyhound races to kill some time. He had one eye on the TV and the other on the main entrance to the second floor. Twice he was asked by blokes if they could take an empty chair from his table. When he was asked a third time, this time by a young woman, Matthewson told her the last empty chair at the table was spoken for. It was just after six. He heard a few loud cheers coming from the gaming tables and when he turned around to see what the ruckus was about Chelsea Wynwood was standing in front of him.

"Are you Dennis?" she asked.

"Even if I wasn't I'd say I was." He was surprised he came up with such a good line.

Matthewson stood up and shook her hand. Both were as nervous as a pair of two-year-olds being led into the Flemington starting gate for their first race.

"Please sit down," Matthewson said.

"This feels like a blind date, don't you think?" he asked.

Chelsea nodded. "I hope you're not disappointed," he said.

"Not at all. You're kinda cute."

"Must be the lighting, or lack of it," Matthewson replied.

"And how about you Dennis. Are you disappointed?"

"Disappointed? I'm ecstatic. You are gorgeous, just gorgeous."

"Thank you. I might have overdone it a bit with the make-up and this," she said pointing to her blue top which barely covered her breasts.

"Nah," Matthewson said. He caught a glimpse of her long legs and touched his bottom lip to make sure he wasn't drooling. Never in his 42 years had he ever been out with a more beautiful woman.

"Can I get you a drink Sarah?"

"Yes please. A glass of chardonnay."

Matthewson looked back at Sarah while he waited at the bar for a bartender to take his order. Part of him was worried that some bloke would sit down next to her while he was gone and snatch her away. It happened to him several years ago, not once, but twice.

Not this time. He returned to their table with Sarah's glass of wine and a beer for himself.

He held up his glass. "Here's to a good night."

"To a good night," she said, touching her glass to his.

After a few moments of uncomfortable silence, Sarah spoke first.

"What made you pick my ad?" Dennis. "Mine was one of the few without a photo."

"Good question. Maybe I wanted to be surprised."

"And are you?"

"I'm stunned actually."

"Why is that?"

"'Cause you are better than anything I could have imagined."

"Thank you. That's sweet."

"I'm a little nervous. I've never done this before," Matthewson admitted.

Sarah reached out and touched his hand. "That's okay. I'll take good care of you," she said with a wink.

"Should we talk business first? Get it out of the way?" Matthewson asked.

"If you want. It's $225 for an hour. That okay?"

"Yes, that's about what I thought it would be."

"So what do you do for a living?" she asked.

Matthewson had thought about what he'd say if the subject came up. A golf pro? A council worker? A salesman? He looked at Sarah, who genuinely seemed interested, and decided to tell the truth. "I work for a local publishing firm. I edit and proofread manuscripts."

"That must be interesting."

"It is. I enjoy it. I had the afternoon off today and came here to play a round of golf."

"I've never played golf."

"You should try it. It's a great way to spend an afternoon. When you're on the course nothing else matters."

"I'd need some lessons."

"Well it just so happens that I give golf lessons on the side for a bit of extra income."

"Oh? And how much do you charge?"

"Two hundred and twenty-five dollars an hour. But it's negotiable."

Sarah laughed. *He's a bit older than me and okay looking, and funny. I wouldn't mind meeting someone like him back home*, she thought. *But he'd probably run if I told him I clean toilets on the* Spirit *and have a three-year-old.*

When Sarah finished her drink, Matthewson suggested they leave and grab some dinner.

"I hear there's a very good buffet here. That okay with you?"

Sarah nodded. "Do you ever play the pokies or blackjack?" she asked as they walked past the gaming tables and machines.

"I did earlier."

"Oh? And how did you do?"

"I did okay. My winnings will pay for dinner."

"And cover my fee?"

"You could say that," Matthewson replied.

Sarah turned several heads on the way out including a security guard who was posted at the entrance to the gaming area. Matthewson noticed. *Feels good to be with the prettiest woman in the resort*, he thought.

Over dinner Dennis never asked Sarah if escorting work was all she did to pay her bills or for how long she had been doing it. *She'll tell me if she wants to.*

However, he did ask where she was from.

"Your ad said you were just in town for two nights."

Chelsea had wondered what she would say if asked. It would have been easy to say Hobart which was less than three hours away. But she went with the truth. "I live in Devonport."

"I've taken the *Spirit* over to Melbourne a couple of times. You ever been on it?" Dennis asked.

"Once in a while. I have family in Melbourne." She didn't want to lie but she was ashamed to tell him the truth.

"And please call me Chelsea. Sarah is my working name."

One lie, one truth. That evens things out, Chelsea said to herself. She wanted to believe that but didn't.

With dinner, dessert and coffee out of the way, the awkward part of the evening arrived.

Chelsea broke the ice.

"Want to come back to my place?" she asked with a seductive smile.

"I guess we could do that."

"We're nearly there," she said after a bit of a hike down several corridors. Her feet were beginning to ache since she didn't wear heels very often. "Here we are," she finally said pointing to the room. She took the card for the room from her purse and unlocked the door.

"You ever stay in the hotel?" Chelsea asked as she flicked on the lights.

"No. But it's pretty nice," he said looking around. The room had a nice view of the golf course. The resort's outdoor lights were sparkling.

Chelsea didn't want to ask, but everything she had read and watched about the escort business talked about getting the money from a client before going to bed.

Matthewson was one step ahead of her. He handed her $225.

"Thank you," she said.

They looked at each other for a moment.

"A couple of the girls in their ads mentioned that kissing was part of the package. Do you kiss your clients?" Matthewson asked.

"Only the ones I like."

"Do you like me?"

Chelsea put her arms around Matthewson and gave him a long, slow kiss.

"That answer your question?" she asked.

Matthewson nodded.

"I'm just going into the bathroom for a second. Don't go anywhere," Chelsea said playfully.

"I wouldn't leave if the fire alarm and sprinklers came on."

When she returned Chelsea told Matthewson to sit on the bed. She removed her top and skirt and stood before him in a lacy black bra and panties. She kept her heels on. "What do you think?"

Matthewson didn't say a word. The lump in his pants did his talking for him. Chelsea undressed him and laid him on his back. She undid her bra, got on top of him and leaned over and kissed him harder than before. She couldn't believe how wet she was. She grabbed the condom she had earlier placed on the bedside table, put it on Matthewson and slowly took him inside her. In less time than it took to run 1200 metres down the Flemington straight, Matthewson had run his race. Chelsea dismounted and laid beside him.

Matthewson said one word when he caught his breath. "Wow".

Chelsea turned to him. "That was nice. Ready for another go?" she asked. "We do have 40 minutes left."

"Give me a couple of minutes. I'm 42 not 22," Matthewson said.

Chelsea laughed. She got up and grabbed two bottles of water from the room's small fridge.

She tossed one to him. "This will help your recovery," she said.

The encore performance featured Matthewson on top. Since he wasn't as nervous and excited as the first time, he was able to hold out longer.

"That was better than I could have ever imagined," Matthewson whispered in her ear as he held her from behind.

"Get your money's worth?"

"Best $225 I've ever spent."

"Do you have any other clients tonight?" Matthewson asked.

"Not as of a couple of hours ago. Let me check my phone."

Completely nude, Chelsea got out of bed and retrieved the cheap phone from her bag.

Matthewson watched intently. It was an image he wanted to keep in his mind for the rest of his life.

"Someone wants to see me at 10pm," Chelsea lied.

"What if I make you a better offer?" Matthewson said as he sat up in bed. He picked up his underwear from the floor and put them on.

"Go on." Chelsea said.

"What if I gave you another $500 to spend the night here. Would that change your mind about that other appointment?"

"Editors and proofreaders make that much money?"

"Some do. If they're lucky."

"What do you mean?"

Matthewson told her about his afternoon on the punt. From the race at Bendigo to his wins at the roulette wheel and blackjack table.

"Most would have gone on with it and lost all their winnings, and more," Chelsea said.

"Most. But I'm not greedy. What do you say? It's the casino's money, not mine."

"Well, since you put it that way. Okay. We have a deal Dennis."

Matthewson took $500 dollars from his wallet, held it up to Chelsea and placed it in her bag. "Excuse me for a moment. A bathroom break."

Matthewson closed the door, went to the toilet, flushed and washed up. He hung a white hand towel on the back of the bathroom door and opened it.

"So where were we?" he asked as he climbed back into bed.

Matthewson left Chelsea's room just after 10 the next morning. He had a golf game with a couple of mates at 11 at Launceston Golf Club and needed to go home and change.

"Would you like to do this again next time you're in town?" he asked.

"That would be nice."

He kissed her on the cheek, thanked her for a lovely evening and left.

An hour later Chelsea got a call from a potential client, and thirty minutes later received another. Both wanted to see a photo before making an appointment.

She texted each a pic and her hourly price and within a minute – like there was any doubt – they each booked appointments. The first was for 12 noon, the second for 3:30pm.

At 12 on the dot there was a knock on her door. She opened it and saw a bloke her father's age standing in front of her. Decades of beer and fast food meant that Elston Shaw's belly arrived everywhere five minutes before he did.

"You're even prettier than your photo," he said, "You gonna let me come in or are we going to do it here in the hallway?" he crudely joked.

Reluctantly Chelsea opened the door.

"Hi. I'm Sarah. Like I said in the text message it's $225 for the hour – paid up front."

Elston Shaw pulled a wad of bills from his pocket, peeled off $225 and handed it to her. "The clock starts now?"

"It does. Make yourself comfortable," Chelsea said pointing to the newly-made bed.

"Would you like me to wear anything special?" she asked.

"What you have on is fine. It's just going to come off anyways, right?"

"It will. I'll be just a minute."

Chelsea ducked into the bathroom and felt like throwing up. "I've been with some losers in my day but this one takes the cake," she said looking at herself in the mirror. She took a deep breath and walked back into the room. Elston Shaw was under the covers and his clothes were on the floor next to the bed.

"Can you do a little striptease? Shake your titties for me?"

"Whatever you want."

Chelsea's removed her top first and then her tight jeans. She wiggled her arse at him, then seductively removed her bra. She shook her breasts for him as he had asked and climbed onto the bed. "This is bloody great. My wife thinks I'm at Bunnings." He laughed loudly and cleared the phlegm from his throat with several coughs.

Maybe he'll die right here and now, and I won't have to go through with this, she thought.

But Elston Shaw was very much alive. He motioned for her to come closer. "C'mere. Let me suck on those nice titties of yours."

Chelsea straddled him and closed her eyes as he sucked her nipples.

"Don't bite them," she said.

Chelsea wasn't sure Shaw heard him. He just kept on going, putting one breast in his mouth and then the other. *At least he hasn't asked me to kiss him.* Luckily for her sake, he didn't.

"I want you to ride me. My wife never does that, never does anything for me more than once a month."

At least I won't have to have that pile of goo on top of me, Chelsea thought.

She pulled back the doona and sheet, grabbed a condom and put it on him.

"Do we really have to use a condom?" he asked.

"It's the law," Chelsea said.

"Damn government. They're even in our bedrooms now."

Chelsea manoeuvred herself to get in position and slid down on top of him. She was sure he wouldn't last long considering how hard he was breathing, coughing and wheezing. But he kept going and going and then flipped her over to finish. He rolled off of her when he did and tried to catch his breath.

"You okay?" Chelsea asked.

He nodded.

"Let me get you some water," she said.

She first grabbed a towel to wipe his sweat off her and returned with a glass of water.

"Thanks hun. Shit, this wouldn't be a bad way to go, would it?" he asked. He took a few sips of water. His breathing slowly returned to normal, or whatever normal is for a man well over 130 kilograms. "I'd love to see the look on me wife's face when she found out I done died in a hooker's bed."

"You're not going to die Elston. You just needed to catch your breath."

Chelsea picked his clothes up from the floor and laid them on the bed. "Thank you," he said.

As he got dressed Chelsea put her bra and panties on.

"How much time we have left?" Shaw asked.

"About 20 minutes."

"Good. What do you say we do it again?"

A cold chill went through Chelsea's body. *Again?*

"Just kidding hun. I won't be able to get another hard-on for a week."

Shaw looked at his watch as he buckled his trousers. He slid his feet into a pair of large brown shoes. Bending over to tie a pair of shoelaces was an impossibility. "I better get my arse over to Bunnings," he said. "The wife wants to do some gardening this afternoon."

"What's she planting?"

"A lot of green shit she wants me to start eating."

"It won't be that bad."

"Oh yes it will. A good thing Bunnings has those sausage sizzles. I'll have one when I get there and another on the way home."

Chelsea smiled. "Take care of yourself Elston."

"You too hun."

Shaw gave Chelsea a small peck on the cheek and left.

Chelsea closed the door behind him, locked it and sprinted to the bathroom.

She spent the next 20 minutes under a hot shower.

Waiting for her hair to dry, Chelsea checked in with her mother and told her she would come by her place tomorrow around lunchtime. "How's Jasmine?" she asked.

"Other than missing her mum she's fine. Your father and I are doing are best to keep her entertained. We just got back from the park and Jazz fell asleep a second after we walked in the door."

"Sleep is just what I need. I'm exhausted. Thanks for looking after her Mum. I really appreciate it. Tell Jazz Mum misses her. See you tomorrow."

Chelsea looked at several pictures of Jazz on her phone and felt her eyes fill with tears. "I'm sorry I'm not there with you sweetheart. But I'm doing this for us." She kissed one of the photos, put her phone in her bag, got dressed and went downstairs for a bite to eat.

Chelsea bought a sandwich and soft drink from a snack bar and went to sit outside in the sun.

A perfect day for golf. I wonder how Dennis's game is going, she thought.

She felt like texting him and saying hello but decided not to. It was just business. Or was it? *He's got my number. If he calls, he calls.*

She checked the time on her work phone before she put it back in her bag. It was 2:10. Time to go back upstairs and get ready for her next appointment which was less than an hour away.

Chelsea received a surprise when she stepped into her room. The room had been made up in her absence. New towels were left at the foot of the bed.

She put on the same outfit she had worn for Dennis in the hope that luck would strike twice.

It didn't. Chelsea didn't like the look of her 3pm appointment from the moment she opened her door. For a moment she thought about shutting it in his face and locking it. He was tall, about 30, a bit overweight with short-cropped hair. He was wearing a tight-fitting t-shirt to show off his tattoos which covered both arms. His jeans were baggy and dirty. She was surprised he got past security downstairs.

"Hi. I'm Sarah. You must be Glenn."

"I am." He looked her over, walked behind her and looked at her again. "Nice outfit."

"Thanks." She paused. "Like I said in the text message. It's $225 up front for the hour. Condoms are a must and there's no kissing."

Glenn took three one-hundred-dollar bills from his pocket and handed them to her. "Keep the change," he said. He sat down in the only chair in the room. "Let's see what you got. Take it all off."

She did as he asked and stood before him wearing just her panties and heels.

"Not bad."

He came at her and pushed her up against the wall, pinning her arms over her head.

"I sure hope you like it rough, because I do."

"I don't," Chelsea screamed. "Stop please."

Glenn smacked her across the face. "You want another?"

Chelsea felt her mouth fill with blood. "No," she yelled.

Glenn took his belt off and used it to tie Chelsea's hands together.

"Turn around and bend over," he yelled at her. He needed both hands to take off his pants and when he let go of her for just an instant, Chelsea pulled her right knee back and thrust it into his groin. He collapsed in front of her, screaming in agony. Chelsea then kicked him in the head and ran into the bathroom. She locked the door and grabbed her work phone which she had left near the sink She was trembling. *If I call the police, my name will be splattered everywhere. Shit. What do I do?* she thought.

She rang Dennis Matthewson, who was having a beer with his mates after playing 18 holes at Launceston Golf Club. He heard crying on the other end of the line.

"Is that you Chelsea? What's going on? What's wrong."

"Help me Dennis, please. Some guy is in my room trying to kill me. I've locked myself in the bathroom."

"He's what?"

"He's trying to kill me. Help me Dennis, please. I want to see my little girl again."

"I'll get help and be there as soon as I can."

"What's going on mate?" asked Charlie Spikes, a member of his foursome.

"Long story. I've got to run."

Thinking quickly, like a veteran cop in the many novels he read, Matthewson rang the resort and asked for security. "It's an emergency," he yelled.

Two rings later Doug King picked up the phone on his desk.

"Security. King speaking."

"Mate, there's an assault in progress in room 276. A woman is being beaten and has locked herself in the bathroom. Please get over there right away."

"Who's this?"

"Never mind who I am, get over there now. If you don't, I'll ring the cops. I don't think your bosses want to see cops running into the resort on a busy Saturday afternoon. You have my number. Call me later. Just get to room 276, NOW."

King bolted from his desk and ran out of his office. A former rugby player who was hired for his muscle, he grabbed two security guards on the second floor and told them to follow him.

"What's going on Doug?" one of them asked.

"A woman is being assaulted in her room."

It took less than a minute for them to reach room 276. King loudly knocked on the door. "Security," he yelled, "Open the door now". When there was no answer King grabbed a pass key he kept in his shirt pocket and opened the door. He saw a big unit rolling on the floor in pain and heard crying coming from the bathroom. "Cuff this bastard and give him a belt with the stick if he plays up," King told Brad Nessler and Casey Hawkins.

King knocked on the bathroom door. "Ma'am, this is Doug King from security. It's safe to come out now. We have the guy in handcuffs. He won't hurt you."

"How can I be sure?"

"It's safe. I promise. We're taking the guy away."

King looked at Nessler and Hawkins. "Take him downstairs. Quietly. Use the elevator and keep him cuffed until I get there."

Chelsea opened the bathroom door a few inches and burst into tears when she saw King. She had a towel wrapped around her and her mouth was bleeding.

"Is he gone?"

"Yes. We have him in custody."

"Are you okay?" King asked looking at Chelsea's bloody mouth.

"I think so. No teeth are loose. He gave me a couple of smacks and then I kicked him in the balls."

"Do you know the man who did this to you?"

"No. He must have followed me."

"Did he rob you?"

"No. He sexually assaulted me. It was awful. He took my clothes off, tied my hands together with his belt and then tried to rape me."

Shit, King thought. *An attempted rape of a customer? This won't look good.*

"We'll have a look at the closed-circuit cameras. That will tell us everything."

"I don't want the police brought into this. I just want to go home. Please."

"Are you sure?" King asked. "If he tried to rape you ..."

"I'm sure. I just want to get my things and go home."

"When did you check in?"

"Last night. I was going to stay tonight too. I came for the country music show."

"I'll get the hotel to give you a full refund for your room and for your tickets".

"Thank you."

"We'll have your name and details at the front desk, and we'll get in touch with you if we need you for anything further. Please accept my apology on behalf of the resort."

As King was walking out of the room Dennis Matthewson came running in.

"Chelsea, what happened?" He saw her bloody mouth. "Who did this to you?"

"I'm not sure. Some guy must have followed me back to the room after I had lunch."

"Jesus."

Matthewson held her tight. "It's alright now sweetheart."

"Excuse me," Doug King asked Matthewson. "What's your relationship with this woman."

"I'm her boyfriend. I'm the one who called you. Can you give us a few minutes? You have my number."

"I'll ring you if we need anything," King said, slowly closing the door behind him.

Chelsea looked up at Matthewson.

"Did you just say you were my boyfriend?"

"I guess I did. Do you want to be my girlfriend?"

Chelsea wanted to kiss Dennis, but her bloody lip and mouth hurt too much. Instead, she hugged him so tight he thought one of his ribs would crack.

"Let's get you cleaned up. You can spend the night at my place if you want."

"I do. And I want you to know something."

"Okay."

"Sarah doesn't exist anymore. I am never doing that again, never."

Dennis smiled. "Good," he said. "I have one question though."

Uh oh, Chelsea thought. *I told him I wanted to see my little girl again. He's going to ask about Jasmine.*

"Want to play a round of mini golf tomorrow?"

Chelsea smiled. "I'd love to."

Colonoscopy

I t may be the most vile, revolting, and disgusting concoction ever designed for human consumption and Mark Bridges had to drink not one, not two, but three tall glasses of the powdery mixture over the next six hours.

He opened the packet and took a brief sniff to se if the taste had improved in the two years since his last colonoscopy. It hadn't. But at least there wasn't a huge pitcher of the crap to down this time; just three large glasses.

With plenty of free time on his hands due to a recent redundancy from the accounting firm he had worked for 27 years, Bridges had booked himself in for his bi-annual colonoscopy. His dad had a small touch of colon cancer about 20 years before he passed away. His surgeons said they had gotten it all and it never troubled him again. But with a history of colon cancer in the family, Bridges' GP made sure he had one every two years. And the day for it was tomorrow, Tuesday.

With the deadline of the first dose rapidly approaching, the 57-year-old Bridges plunked the powder into a glass, filled it with cold water, stirred it several times and looked at it. Getting it down without his breakfast coming up was the first challenge.

Standing over the kitchen sink just in case, he took the first sip of the slightly orange-flavoured mixture and shuddered.

"This is fucking horrible," he shouted. After taking a deep breath he took a longer drink of the putrid liquid and then polished the rest of it off, slamming the glass down on the kitchen table when it was finally empty.

"One down, two more to go," he said loudly.

There was no one asking him how he was travelling. Bridges had been on his own since a long relationship with a friend of a friend ended half-a-dozen years earlier.

At least four glasses of water or some other approved drink to combat the dehydration was next on the menu. If only he had bought some Gatorade on the way home.

It was too late to go out now and he did not want to bother one of his neighbours. The wheels of his digestive system were in motion, and they could not be put on hold.

Now ordinarily a cool glass of water would be easy to down. Anyone could do it. Even his elderly neighbour, John, who had to ingest everything through a straw. But four straight glasses? It was a chore. Bloated and exhausted after downing glass number four, Bridges sat down in his favourite chair and waited for the anal fireworks to begin. His appointment was at 11:10 the following morning and Bridges was hopeful that the flushing of his toilet would cease by midnight.

Two years ago, he flushed the same toilet 36 times and went through a roll and a half of three-ply toilet paper.

By the last flush he was afraid the bloody toilet handle would come off from overuse. It was nearly a world record – 36 flushes – a woman from the Guiness Book of World Records said.

The record is held by a somewhat portly fellow who won last year's Independence Day hot dog eating contest at Coney Island, Brooklyn in the US.

Not content with eating just the dogs, the fuckwit had put mustard and sauerkraut on them. He won the contest and a year's supply of hot dogs but did not leave his bathroom until the afternoon of July 8 and passed away the following morning.

An overdose of sauerkraut was the official cause of death according to coroner Clay Mitchell, who was immediately relieved of his duties by the New York City Health Department and placed on paid leave.

Mitchell celebrated his unplanned paid holiday by taking his family to Coney Island. "Is this a great country or what?" he boasted to his wife and two young children before boarding the Cyclone without them. His wife and kids were afraid to go on the roller coaster.

At its uppermost point, Mitchell lifted the safety bar, attempted to take a selfie, and fell to his death from the historic wooden roller coaster which opened on June 26, 1927. He became the coaster's fourth victim.

The middle-aged woman he landed on, who was wearing a Make America Great Again t-shirt with Donald Trump's picture plastered on the front and back, became victim number five.

As the remaining passengers were safely take off the cyclone by Coney Island staff and emergency personnel, it became clear to Clay's wife, Courtney, that he was the one who had been ejected from the ride.

Sobbing uncontrollably and holding her two kids by their hands, Courtney was escorted to the area where her late husband and the Trump backer were mashed together and covered by a green tarpaulin. As the tarpaulin was lifted by a police officer, Courtney let out a massive scream.

After her crying subsided, she lifted her head from the chest of the policer officer who was consoling her and asked, "Will I get any of his paid leave money?"

"You'll get plenty more than that with a good lawyer," the copper said.

At the sound of those promising words, Courtney's tears and sobbing were immediately replaced by a smile longer than the Cyclone itself.

It was just before midnight when Bridges made his last disposal of the evening. He trudged off to bed, his sore and raw arse aching and was asleep within five minutes. He was up 90 minutes later and another two hours after that to finish the evacuation job that was into its 14th hour.

Remembering not to eat or drink anything when he awoke, Bridges showered, got dressed, had a look at the morning paper and took the train and tram into one of the city's better hospitals.

He arrived at 10:45am. His appointment was for 11:10. After a short wait he heard his name called out and took a seat with a nurse who asked him a laundry list of questions.

"Do you have any metal objects in you? Do you have a pacemaker? Are you an intravenous drug user? Have you been out of the country in the last two weeks?"

"No, no, no and no."

"Is it true that your partner is leaving you just as soon as she recovers her eyesight?"

"Huh", Bridges said with a puzzled look on his face. Once he realised, she was joking, he laughed.

"Just checking if you were paying attention," the nurse said.

She was pleasant enough, in her early 30s he guessed, just not his type. A bit rough around the edges and a tad overweight.

She rolled up his sleeve to check his blood pressure and much to his surprise it was a perfect 122 over 78. She then took his temperature with a new device that barely touched his forehead. Again, near perfect. 36.7. His weight was an even 79kg, which included his shoes and clothing.

"Now follow me," she said. They walked down a long corridor to a bunch of cubicles. She unlocked one of the doors. Bridges was told to take off all his clothes – everything – and then to put on a cloth gown with the opening at the back. A white robe and disposable cloth slippers finished off the ensemble.

"When you're done," the nurse said, "put all your things in this basket and go to the waiting room. The anaesthetist will call you when it is your turn. Good luck."

Bridges shut the door and got undressed, the blue gown on – with the opening at the back – then the white robe, which resembled something you would get at a classy hotel or an upmarket massage parlour. The slippers were next. With all his belongings packed into the small plastic basket, he extended its handles, picked it up and walked to the waiting room where four men and one woman were seated. They all had on the same blue gown, white robe, and cloth slippers.

"Looks like we all shop at the same store," Bridges said as he took a seat.

One of the men smiled and another adjusted himself to keep his merchandise out of sight. The other two couldn't be bothered looking up from their phones. The woman let out an uncomfortable laugh. She was the next one called, the attendant taking her basket and escorting her into the operating theatre.

Bridges picked up a golf magazine with a picture of someone who looked like Lee Trevino on it.

How old was this magazine anyways? Only 18 years, par for a hospital waiting room I suppose.

"Golf is a good walk spoiled," Mark Twain once wrote.

Perhaps, but when you send a tee shot 250 metres down the centre of the fairway or hit an iron to within two feet of the cup or sink a putt from 20 metres, there is not a better feeling on earth; unless it's your divorce attorney ringing to say your ex doesn't want anything.

Bridges lifted his head when he heard his name called by the anaesthetist. Holding a clipboard, he motioned for Bridges to follow him into a small office. "Leave the basket," he said.

The anaesthetist looked to be in his 50s; tall, dark-haired, clean shaven and not overly enthused. He had probably put 30 or 40 people under since his first patient at 7am.

"Allergies?" he asked.

"Penicillin," Bridges answered although he couldn't be 100 percent sure. It was one of those things that your mother told you when you finally left home for good. But better to be safe than sorry, so he always answered penicillin when asked.

It was better than getting on the phone to his 90-year-old mother and asking her about it.

"What's wrong? You're going in for a what? When? Where?" she would start shrieking.

After his request to have the IV inserted into his arm instead of the top of his hand, which hurt like a motherfucker and left a nasty mark, was refused, Bridges walked back to the waiting room to wait. And wait some more. Two had gone into surgery in his brief absence leaving a cosy group of four.

Bridges had overheard a lot of weird phone conversations over the last few years but the next was about to make its way to the top of the list.

The phone of the bloke sitting next to him started to ring. He pulled it out. From where, Bridges did not want to know.

"That's alright mate." Silence followed and then came the corker. "Listen, I'm about to have a colonoscopy. Yeah, a colonoscopy. So, I'll get back to you."

Bridges' name was called next. He knew the drill; hand the basket to the nurse and walk into the theatre where he as greeted by the anaesthetist.

"Lay down on your left side please with your right arm extended and relax," he was told.

He felt the doctor's hand looking for a vein.

"Now you'll feel a little prick."

With the needle firmly in place and his hand throbbing, Bridges gastroenterologist sauntered over and took a seat on a stool facing him. A tall, distinguished, good-looking man with a full head of wavy hair and a pair of trendy glasses, Dr Kinsey had a good bedside manner. He uttered a friendly hello, looked at his clipboard, and then Bridges said, as he always did, "You're looking well Mark."

Well? Bridges said to himself. *Hardly. I haven't eaten a full meal in about 36 hours and spent the better part of the previous evening in the crapper. I'm also half asleep on an operating table wearing a flimsy gown with my raw and red arse full exposed.*

The last words he heard before drifting off were those of the anaesthetist. "Count backwards from 99 please."

Bridges came to less than an hour later in a reclining chair, the IV still firmly stuck in his hand and farting like he was an extra in the campfire scene from *Blazing Saddles*.

He wondered how he got from the operating table into the recliner but drew a blank. *Maybe it's better not to know,* he thought as a nurse carrying sandwiches and juice pulled back the curtains on both sides of his recliner.

Bridges picked up a sandwich, and unsure of what it was, examined and sniffed it.

"CHOPPED LIVER? IN A CATHOLIC HOSPITAL? Is this some sort of a joke?" he asked the nurse.

"Well, it was either that or gefilte fish, but the chopped liver goes down easier," the nurse said.

Bridges lowered his head. *Everyone is a fucking comedian these days,* he thought.

"Do you have any hot dogs?" Bridges asked. "Oh, and if you do, hold the sauerkraut, okay?"

Eddie

I t's Caulfield Cup Day and Eddie Lawson is $69 ahead before the first race has been run.

You see, Eddie doesn't like to pay for admission – anywhere, even though he can afford to. He hasn't paid to see a movie since *Naked Gun*.

A few weeks earlier, he called in a favour, got his hands on a Channel 7 media vest, and had the run of the MCG at the AFL grand final. When he was approached at quarter time on the boundary by someone from security, he started talking into his fake headset and was left alone.

He's seen Federer and Nadal from the best seats in the house at the Australian Open and wound up at the end of the team bench late last season at a Melbourne United NBL game by masquerading as a physio.

"I've been treating Mulkey's ankle," he told an assistant coach who asked who he was during the warm-ups. "Let's hope you're not needed," he was told. But he was when star guard Chris Mulkey rolled an ankle in the second quarter and limped to the bench.

The trainer was busy taping another player's strained shoulder, so Mulkey was brought to Eddie, who was seated at the end of the team bench. Eddie took off Mulkey's right sneaker and started to work on the injured area. "Any pain mate?" Eddie asked. "None," Mulkey answered.

"None?"

"None, it's my left ankle that's hurt. Who the heck are you anyway?"

With that Eddie took off. He jumped over several seats and sprinted up the aisle. He made his way to the main concourse and then ducked into the first men's toilet he saw. A stall was free and he took it. Eddie turned his black polo shirt inside out, took off the fake moustache he was sporting and shoved it in his pocket. From his other pocket he removed a pair of eyeglasses and put them on. He slicked his dark hair back, took a leak and flushed the toilet. He stuffed his United hat in the trash and watched the rest of the game from an unoccupied seat in the upper level.

Eddie enjoyed other pastimes besides sport in the cultural city of Melbourne; like art. Not wanting to spend half a day waiting in a line at the National Gallery and then paying to see the Van Gogh exhibit a couple of years ago, Eddie purchased a cheap canvas from a two-dollar shop, wrapped it in brown paper, put on a pair of work pants and shirt and marched into the National Gallery armed with just a clipboard. "I was told to bring this right over from the airport. It's for the exhibit," he told a befuddled security guard. "Just sign here and I'll be on my way." The guard signed his name, Eddie handed him the canvas, took back the clipboard and lost himself in the crowd. "A fine exhibit," he told people waiting in line as he exited two hours later.

"This just came, Mr Worthington," an out-of-breath gallery worker said as he handed Eddie's package to the gallery's assistant director. "A courier brought it from the airport. He said it is part of the Van Gogh exhibition."

Worthington took the canvas and looked at it suspiciously. "Everything that we were expecting is here. What is this?"

He tore the brown wrapping paper from the canvas and gazed at it. It had a $4.99 sticker on the front and a Made in Amsterdam sticker on the back. "Is this your idea of a joke?" Worthington angrily asked the fellow who delivered it. "Because it is not fucking funny."

"It's not my joke," Bill Monet said. "Security asked me to bring this to you."

"Get out of here," Worthington said. "And take this damn thing with you," he said flinging the canvas in Monet's direction. An art student, Monet picked it up and stuck it under his arm. *I can use this*, he thought. He put it in the locker he shared with three others and returned to work answering queries from patrons.

An out-of-work accountant, 42-year-old Eddie Lawson wasn't in dire need of a job thanks to the bundle his father left him several years ago. "Just don't blow it on the horses," Harold Lawson told him when he visited his dad one winter afternoon in a nearby nursing home. Four months later Harold Lawson was gone. Two weeks after his father's funeral a sizeable six-figure sum was dropped into his savings account. Eddie paid his rent for the next six months on his modest one-bedroom unit in Caulfield and started to spend less and less time at work and more and more time at the racetracks in the Melbourne area. He took the train to Geelong and Warrnambool, drove out to Mornington and as far as Echuca. He wasn't a bad handicapper which meant he just about broke even.

But as Caulfield Cup Day approached, Eddie was in the midst of a long losing streak. His last big winner had been on Cox Plate Day several years ago when he backed European galloper Adelaide to win the 2400m Group 1. He put five grand on the animal at the fixed odds of $7 and walked out of Moonee Valley and straight into a cab with $35,000 in cash.

The next year he loaded up on Winx, who was running in her first Cox Plate. He put five grand on the mighty mare at the fixed odds of $4. She easily saluted and Eddie again was flush with cash. He took his best mates out that night and dropped over $800 on food and drinks at a Southbank restaurant. Sid Henderson, who he played cricket with more than a decade ago at a local club, not only brought along the gal he was seeing at the time but also one of her girlfriends who she thought would be perfect for Eddie. And she was. The two fell head over heels for each other although Eddie wasn't totally convinced that Chelsea Samuelson felt the same way he did. "She knows I'm on a bit of a lucky streak," he told Sid one Saturday afternoon at a barbecue which Sid hosted. "When the streak ends, and it will, will she still feel the same?" he asked.

"Chelsea's into you, not your money. Gail told me so," Sid said. "She's got a job, her own place, her own money. Don't worry about it. Enjoy the ride. Here," he said, handing Eddie a hot dog. "Stop worrying."

Eddie's hot streak was well and truly behind him, and so was Chelsea Samuelson, when he arrived at Caulfield on cup day in October of 2017. He walked the five long blocks to the track, showed an old guard manning the trainer's parking lot a forged pass and walked straight in, saving himself the $69 admission fee. Eddie had worked day and night studying the form and felt the race favourites would have trouble running out 2400 metres. There were just a handful of European invaders in the $3 million handicap unlike the Melbourne Cup three weeks later where nearly half of the 24-horse field was from overseas.

Eddie settled on a horse from the popular Burrows, Burrows and Coleman team named Boom Box who was 50-1. He didn't make a bet until the cup. Instead, he watched a parade of skirt for a few hours, soaked up some sun and downed a few cold cans of Carlton Brewery's finest.

An hour or so before the cup Eddie walked out of the crowded grandstand to the tie-up stalls at the back of the course where the cup horses were being looked after. Boom Box was not bothered one bit by the big crowd. In fact, he was so relaxed he looked like he was asleep. Eddie watched hall-of-fame trainer David Burrows saddle him up and as he was led to the walking ring by his strapper, Eddie called out to Burrows. "Will he run as good as he looks David?"

"I sure hope so. He shouldn't be 50-1, that's for sure," Burrows said.

Eddie agreed. He looked at his copy of *Best Bets* one last time, just to make sure he hadn't missed anything, and nervously walked over to the betting windows. He preferred betting with the TAB rather than the bookmakers and as he waited on line behind a throng of once-a-year race goers, Eddie reached into his pocket and pulled out $5000 in $100 bills. He took a deep breath, put the five grand on the counter and told the woman behind the window that he wanted $5000 to win on number 13 at the fixed odds of 50-1. The number 13 saddle cloth didn't bother Eddie. He wasn't superstitious. He put the ticket in his left shirt pocket and buttoned it. It was secure as a newborn in its mother's arms.

Eddie watched the race on a big screen TV at the back of the course. He was as nervous as he had ever been at a racetrack as the horses were loaded into the gate. Boom Box broke well from his inside barrier, held his position down the backstretch, hit the lead at the 100m mark and scored by just over a length. Eddie was shaking as he unbuttoned his shirt pocket. He gazed at the ticket, looked at the results on the big screen and checked his ticket yet again. It matched. He took a deep breath and walked inside the members' area of the grandstand. When correct weight was announced he got in line to cash the ticket. Since a 50-1 shot had won the line was not a long one.

When he got to the window Eddie handed the ticket to an older woman behind the counter and watched her eyes light up as the amount of $250,000 appeared on her screen.

"How would you like to be paid sir," she asked. "By cheque or in cash."

Eddie hadn't given that much thought. After a moment he said, "I'll take $25,000 in cash – $100 bills please – and the rest by cheque."

She counted out $25,000 and handed it across the counter.

"I'll be back with the cheque in a moment. Don't go anywhere," she said.

"I won't."

A dapper older fellow wearing a green TAB sports jacket appeared two minutes later. Eddie guessed he was a supervisor of some sort and gave him his name when he was asked. "Is it Eddie or Edward?" the man asked. "Edward please. Edward Lawson. L-a-w-s-o-n."

His name was printed in blue ink. The man then signed his name and handed the cheque to Eddie. He looked at the man's signature. "Samuelson is it?"

"Yes."

"Do you have a daughter named Chelsea?" Eddie asked as he folded the cheque and put it in his shirt pocket.

"Yes I do. How do you know my daughter?" Samuelson asked.

"We dated for a while."

"She never mentioned you."

"Maybe that's because I didn't have 250 large on me at the time. Cheers mate."

Eddie walked to the escalator, rode to the ground floor, and surrounded by hundreds of racegoers, briskly walked out of the gates. Most walked to the train station across the street, ignoring several volunteers from the Salvos and Red Cross, who were rattling their cans.

While Eddie waited in line for a cab – he didn't feel safe walking home with all the cash he had on him – he looked over at one of the volunteers. He looked like his dog had just run away.

"Not many donations coming your way?" Eddie asked.

"There never is when a long shot wins the chocolates."

Eddie reached into his right front pocket, the 25 grand was safely stashed in his left, took a $50 note from his billfold and dropped it in the can."

"That's very kind of you sir. Thank you.

"I had a good day. It's the least I can do."

As he waited for the next cab, Eddie's mobile rang. He retrieved it from his jacket pocket and looked at the number – an unknown caller. Being the curious type, Eddie answered it instead of hanging up. "Eddie Lawson here. Who's calling?"

"Eddie. It's Chelsea, Chelsea Samuelson. I hear you cleaned up on the cup."

Every bone in his body was telling him to hang up. But Eddie, who had not enjoyed the pleasure of any female company for months, replied.

"I did alright," he said.

"Alright? Dad told me you won so much they paid you by cheque."

"Like I said, I did alright."

"Celebrating with anyone?"

"Haven't given it much thought to tell you the truth."

"Want to get together later?"

Eddie thought about it. *Where was she when I was going through that rough patch and needed someone?*

"Eddie? You there?"

He hung up, blocked her number, hopped in a cab, and headed home.

The TAB

'm sitting on a stool at my local TAB, my form guide spread on a round wooden table, a red pen in one hand and a cold beer in the other, when out of the corner of my eye I see Steve Sandberg enter the room from the bistro.

Someone had to have shouted him lunch I figure because "Nails" rarely has enough money on him to buy a can of baked beans let alone a parma. A carpenter, who doesn't work as much as he used to, Steve owes me, and a few other regulars at the TAB, a bit of scratch, and if we all live to be 100, it's doubtful that we'll ever see any of it.

But Steve is such a decent bloke that nobody ever hounds him to pay back his debts. In fact, every now and then they hand him another five or 10-dollar note even though he is the worst handicapper anyone has ever known. In a two-horse race his pick would come third. I myself have handed him more fivers than I can count. But today I'm a bit short of cash thanks to a couple of unforeseen household expenses and I don't have it in me to say, *Sorry mate, you'll have to ask someone else.*

I tug my baseball cap down so low trying not to be seen that I nearly knock my spectacles off my prominent nose. "If my horse had your nose" … some of my mates have been known to say. I've got my head buried so deep in the form guide trying to get an angle on the next at Flemington that I'm sure there's newsprint on the tip of my schnoz.

Despite my attempt to fly under the radar, Steve spots me. "Derek," he yells and instinctively I turn around. He's coming straight towards me, bouncing the form guide from the *Herald Sun* on his hip. Odds are he plucked it out of a trash bin instead of forking over $3 at the newsagent a few doors down.

"Good to see you mate," he says extending his hand.

"You too. You're looking well. Had an early winner?"

"Nah. I was on the $2.50 shot in the last but got run down late. I'm just about tapped out," I tell him.

Steve asks the two people sitting at the table next to us if anyone is using an unoccupied stool. A big, bearded bloke says no and Steve swings it around to join me.

I don't know the name of the bloke, but he may be the smartest of the 30 or so people in the place. He comes for the beer and a chat and not once have I seen him have a wager. He's the owner of the dog out front, a mixed breed who will never claim a prize for best looker at a dog show. The dog is a friendly sort though, is not tied up, never barks, and passes the hours laying under a bench. A bowl of clean water sits there beside him.

"Who do you like in the next?" Nails asks. "Oliver's horse is flying. They're not gonna beat him, are they?"

"Not sure mate. I'm trying to figure it out. He's up in class and the money is coming for him but I'm not convinced."

Before Steve asks if I can loan him a tenner, I tell him I've got just enough on me for another beer, a bet in the next and a quaddie.

"Sorry Steve. I had to pay a plumber $150 this morning to fix my hot-water heater (which is true). Maybe next time."

"I understand," he says dejectedly. "Hope you win enough to pay him."

He gets up from his chair and looks around the room for another mark. "Brian," he calls out to a bloke standing glued to a TV where he's watching the horses in the next at Randwick being loaded into the starting gate. Brian looks up and rolls his eyes when he sees whose coming his way. Brian holds his hand up before Steve even says a word. "If the six horse wins this I'll lend you five bucks, okay?"

Well, it must be Steve's lucky day because the six horse comes like a shot on the outside in the last 50 metres to get up by a half head and pays $14.60 to win and $4.40 to place. Brian has $10 each way on the James Cumming trained horse and collects close to $200. He collects and hands Nails a tenner. "Thanks mate. I'll pay you back."

Sure you will, Brian says to himself. "Don't worry about it, okay? This is a gift. Just like the one I just got. There's no way that horse should have won."

"You're a champion Brian, a champion," Steve says slapping him on the back. He walks over to a quiet corner, puts the $10 note in his pocket, takes out his form guide and flips to the fifth race at Flemington. There's 12 minutes to start time. Trainer Tony Messing's Oval Office Moron is the lukewarm $3.50 favourite in the 11-horse race over 1400 metres. Nails does his best to find someone who can beat the three-year-old gelding but can't. He puts his left hand in the pocket of his jeans just to make sure the $10 note is still there, circles the numbers of three other horses in his form guide and heads to a quiet counter to fill out his betting slips.

Nails puts $5 to win on Oval Office Moron and $5 worth of trifectas and first fours with Moron on top.

I settle on Oval Office Moron as well and as the horses start being loaded into the gate I put my bets down. A tenner on Moron to salute as well as a couple of trifectas.

As the horses jump the sound gets turned up so we can clearly hear race caller Matt Hendricks. The same courtesy is not given to the other tracks conducting meetings today. You've got to stand close to the TVs to listen to the calls from Kembla Grange, Morphettville, The Gold Coast and even Royal Randwick.

Oval Office Moron settles midfield and could not be in a better spot as the field swings for home. His rider peels him out with 400m to go, he hits the front with 200m left and coasts to the line. Despite a bit of bumping in the battle for the minor placings the numbers 4, 8, 1, 6 go up on the screens pretty quickly. I've got the winner of course and the trifecta and I let out a "Yes" when the payouts for the exotics come up. The trifecta of 4, 8 and 1 is paying $312.00 which will net me about $340, my best day in months and that's before the first leg of the quaddie. The plan is to collect and watch the rest of the card at home.

As I wait for correct weight, Matt Hendricks announces that the rider of the fourth-placed horse is claiming interference on the third-placed horse in the closing stages of the race. The head on shots are shown and although the one horse gave the six horse a bit of a bump around the 100m mark I am fairly certain the result will stand considering the one-length margin between the third and fourth-placed horses. Over at another TV in the corner of the room, Nails has not taken his eyes off the screen. He's carefully looked at his tickets and has a 4, 8, 6 trifecta and a 4, 8, 6, 1 first four. "Take the one down, take the one down," he's pleading to no one in particular. Four minutes pass, then five, then six. Finally, 12 minutes after the race was run, Matt Hendricks announces that the protest has been upheld and that the official placings are 4, 8, 6 and 1.

"Shit," I say. "There goes $312 bucks."

I tear up my now worthless trifecta tickets and turn to walk out when I hear a familiar voice scream. "I got it. I got it. Finally."

It's Nails. I scoot over to him and ask what all the hollering is about it.

"I've got the trifecta and the first four. Can you believe it? All because that third-placed horse got DQ'd. It's a fucking miracle."

I look at the screen and do the math. The trifecta of 4, 8 and 6 is paying $580 and the first four over $1300. Son of a gun. He'll pocket close to $2000. As bad as I feel after being DQ'd I feel good for Nails.

He deserved a big win. The question is will he pay back the hundreds of dollars he's borrowed over the last few months.

The answer was never in doubt. Nails finds Brian at the bar and hands him a $50 note. "Thanks mate. I couldn't have done it without you."

Nails hands me $100. "I told you I'd pay you back. I told you."

I didn't have the heart to tell him he owes me another hundred.

Grand Final Day

I t's Grand Final day and no one is happy. The Melbourne, Hawthorn, and Richmond fans – along with one St Kilda supporter – a dozen in all – and several of their better halves – start showing up around 30 minutes before kick-off.

It is me and my wife's turn to host the annual grand final soiree. It is a bitterly cold day and a strong wind from the southwest – a Shackleton I've named it – is bending the branches of the trees on our quiet street. I've got the barbecue going and the smell of the snags, onions and burgers is going down better than the sounds coming from the Black Eyed Peas at the MCG. The only fans at the "G" on their feet are those trying to get some circulation back into their frozen limbs. The suits in the heated private boxes are mingling after their expensive lunches, martinis in their hands, hands which have never had to do a day of hard work in their privileged lives.

The 2:30pm kick-off is 10 minutes away and the stands at the MCG are nearly full.

"Who the hell is West Coast playing?" one of the suits asks another.

"Collingwood."

"Jesus. If Melbourne hadn't been flogged last weekend at least I would have an interest."

"I know what you mean mate. I cancelled my ski trip on the hope that the Dees would be here. They've sure had their highs and lows over the years."

"Yeah? What day was the high?"

The two share a laugh and order another round of drinks.

"What do you say we make it interesting?" the first suit asks.

"A grand?"

"You're on. Who do you want?"

"West Coast. That way I can enjoy watching Eddie and his lads cry after the final siren."

The two shake hands.

"You bring that gal you've been keeping company with?" suit number one asks.

"Couldn't risk it. Had to bring my wife."

"I hear you. Mine's over at the bar finding out who everyone is wearing."

I'm greeting our guests, taking their drink orders as they find a seat around the year-old 50-inch TV. My wife June brings several platters of fruit and appetizers from the kitchen and carefully lays them on the large dining room table. "Help yourselves," she says. Several varieties of chips and dips are laid out on the nearby coffee table.

The last one to arrive, two minutes before the first bounce is Dave Marshall, one of my best mates. He walks in, a Collingwood scarf over his black and white jumper. Dave loves the Pies and reckons Steve Nichols will lead his mob to victory. He heads straight towards the kitchen, takes a brownie from a freshly baked tray and bursts into the living room. "C'mon Pies," he yells. Crumbs fall from his mouth as he does.

"This is bloody delicious," he tells me. "Mind if I have another one."

"No mate. Help yourself."

June sees Dave grab a brownie and runs over to me.

"Are you going to tell him what he's eating?"

"What do you mean? Look at him. He's enjoying himself. Why stop him? He's scarfing it down like a labrador. He loves your cooking."

"It's funny you used the word labrador," June says.

"It is?"

"Yes."

She pulls me aside and tells me the brownies Dave is eating have been specially baked for our 12-week-old golden lab and her friends at puppy school.

"It's dog food?"

"Dog treats."

"What's in it?"

"Chicken livers, eggs, flour. It won't hurt him."

"But it's dog food."

"What's the worst that can happen?" she asks.

At that point Dave got up from his seat. But instead of cheering a goal by Marcus Briggs he headed to the back door, opened it, and stepped out into the chill. He walks past the barbecue which Geordie Howe is manning and heads to the garden where he unzips his fly, urinates on a patch of newly planted tomatoes, and lays down on the soft grass.

Two hours later, as the strains of the West Coast Eagles team song come through the television speakers, Dave is still outside snoring away. His legs are twitching as if he's chasing a thrown stick. June and I move closer, being careful not to disturb him.

"Another brownie," he mumbles softly. "Another brownie."

The Koshers

t began with just two words spoken by a mate of mine – nice hat – and ended with a string of expletives.

My lovely and I decided to have lunch one Sunday with a close friend of ours and his date at a local cafe which had just opened in one of Melbourne's bayside suburbs. The owners had colourful flags and grand opening signs posted on the freshly painted, white-picket fence of an old, converted church and they seemed to be working. A good crowd was already inside and in the adjoining courtyard on the sunny but breezy afternoon when we arrived. Elliott and his female friend – "it's strictly platonic," he told me when we set the lunch date up – had gotten there before Julie and I and had grabbed a table inside.

We spotted the strictly platonic pair at a table next to a large window and made our way to them, dodging a waiter who looked to be about 12. Elliot and I greeted each other with a hug as we always do. He gave Julie a peck on the cheek and then warmly introduced us to Janine, a slim, attractive, dark-haired woman who bore an uncanny resemblance to author Kathy Lette. I guessed she was in her mid-to-late 40s, or about five years younger than Elliott. Julie and I are both on the wrong side of 50 – just – and on most mornings feel our age rather than each other.

Janine is one of those people you meet and after five minutes feel like you have known for 10 years. She slotted into our little group as easy as

Elaine did with Jerry, George, and Kramer. The conversation turned to that day's state election in Victoria; we had all voted in the morning. Only Elliot had voted for the coalition, which judging by the latest polls had as much chance of winning as I had of finding a non-vegetarian dish on the café's menu.

Julie and Janine talked about the upcoming holidays and how much they were looking forward to time off from work while Elliot and I chatted about the recent AFL draft. "What are you guys doing for Christmas?" Janine asked me.

Julie and I don't have any children, unless you count the five-month-old labrador puppy we have at our hair-covered home, and since I am of the Jewish persuasion and Julie is not a fan of the commercialisation of Christmas, the day is a low-key affair.

"We'll probably stay at home and then later on have Chinese food for dinner," I told her.

"Chinese? No. You're coming over to my place for a traditional Christmas dinner."

"We are?" I asked.

"Yes. It's my turn to host this year. You'll like my brothers and sisters and their kids. We always have a lot of fun."

I turned to Julie, who was sitting next to me. She lightly shrugged her shoulders. "Alright then. We'll be there, thank you," I told Janine.

"That's very nice of you to invite us," Julie added.

I looked across the table to Elliot. "You'll be there mate?" I asked.

"He's got other plans," Janine said. "Don't you Elliot?"

"Yes," Elliot said looking a bit uncomfortable. "Christmas dinner with my sisters and brother and nieces and nephews, and then the Boxing Day test on Wednesday."

"What about stopping by Janine's for a drink after dinner?" I asked.

"Can't mate. Too busy."

I was a bit perplexed by Elliot's lack of enthusiasm, but it became clearer when he went to the toilets after our meals and before our coffees and deserts arrived.

"I hope I'm not being too forward Janine, but I'm a curious person and I need to ask. What's the deal with you and Elliot? You seem to like him so why is your friendship just platonic and not anything more?"

"It's his idea," she said. "I'm keen but he isn't."

Julie and I looked at each other and then looked at Janine. Seated across from us was a very attractive, unmarried woman with no kids. Why would Elliot want to spend time with her but not get involved? I asked him that when Julie used the toilets before we left the cafe.

"She's just not my type pal. Let's leave it at that, okay?"

And we did. After sorting the bill, the four of us got up and walked to the exit. As we said our goodbyes on the footpath, a couple walked past us on the way in.

"Nice hat," Elliot said to the man, who was wearing a colourful cap.

"Thank you," he said. "It's a Sephardic yarmakuh I bought when I was in Israel."

"That's interesting," Elliot said. "A mate of mine ..."

Sensing that this could go on for an hour, Janine gave Elliot a nudge with her elbow. "We've really got to get going," she said pointing to her watch.

And they did, leaving Julie and I standing there with the couple.

The fellow was about 60 and had a thatch of gray hair under his yarmakuh. His wife was a tall drink of water and perhaps a few years younger.

"How about a yarmakuh like that for you hun?" Julie cheekily asked me.

The fellow perked up. "Are you Jewish? Have you ever been to Israel?" he asked.

Julie's comment, coupled with my large nose, had given me away. I'm Jewish but not the religious type. I was bar mitzvahed when I was 13 but avoided synagogue religiously.

"I never have been to Israel and probably won't," I told the fellow. "I'm just not religious."

"You don't observe Shabbat?

"No, I don't."

He looked disappointed.

"Well, it was nice meeting you. Enjoy your lunch. The food here is very good," I told him and his better half.

Julie and I had a walk around town, gazing at the shop windows. We picked up some apples and a rock melon at a fruit and veg shop which surprisingly was open and bought a pair of gardening gloves at a two-dollar shop to replace the pair our dog had chewed. We walked back to the other end of the shopping strip where our car was parked only to run into the Jewish couple from earlier.

"How was lunch?" I asked.

"We'd go back," the woman said.

"I guess we will too," Julie answered.

"We should have lunch together. Next Sunday work for you?" the fellow asked. He extended his hand. "By the way I am David and this is Monica," he said pointing to the Empire State Building next to him.

"I'm Benjamin, this is Julie."

We shook hands all around.

"Next Sunday would be fine," Julie said. "Same cafe. Around one good for you?"

David and Monica each nodded their heads. "One would be fine," David said.

"Alright. One it is. Sorry to run but we've left our puppy outside on her own today for the first time, so we need to get back home."

"What kind of dog?" Monica asked, her head partially obscured by low clouds.

"A golden lab," Julie said.

David and I exchanged mobile numbers and we got on our way.

"Lunch with them ought to be fun, eh?" Julie asked when we reached the safety of our Toyota.

"Why do I get the feeling it is going to be like a trip to the dentist?"

Three days later I got a text message from David.

"Hi Benjamin. Would you and Julie like to come over to our house on Saturday to celebrate Shabbat?

It took me a few minutes to remember what Shabbat was. I'm sorry to admit I had to Google it. Somewhere my old rabbi wept.

Google gave me the following information: Shabbat is observed from a few minutes before sunset on Friday evening until the appearance of three stars in the sky on Saturday night and is ushered in by lighting candles and reciting a blessing.

"Candles? A blessing? Aww, prairie shit."

I showed Julie the message. "Shabbat? What is that?"

I told her how I had to Google it and then explained what it was.

"Not knowing what Shabbat is, is like me not knowing what a baptism. I'm a shiksa, right?" she asked.

"I'm pretty sure it's shiska," I answered.

"Well, whatever it is we're in for one fun afternoon," I sarcastically said.

I texted him back saying we'd be delighted to come and if we should bring anything.

"Wonderful", was the reply. "Come by around 4. We're on Jerusalem Drive, number 36. We keep a kosher home so please do not bring anything."

A kosher home? No meat? No chicken? No ice cream or dairy products? I wouldn't last a day. I wondered if there was such a thing as kosher beer.

I cursed Elliot. "Why did he have to say, 'nice hat'? Why couldn't he have just said good afternoon like anyone else and kept on walking? I should send the Koshers over to his place.

After the Saturday afternoon Shabbat celebration, which featured a reading from the Torah and a lecture on the importance of Judaism, which we sat through with smiles frozen on our faces, the shiska and I decided we had to put an end to this burgeoning friendship.

"I think we've got them," David told Monica after we had left. "Rabbi Glickstein is going to be so pleased. Two more into his flock. All we need is another two couples and we'll win that trip to Bali."

We kept our lunch date the next afternoon, found a table for four and ordered. They each had a vegetarian dish while we ordered the fish and chips and a burger with the lot. It was not meant to offend them, it's just what we felt like having. Earlier they had told us it was okay for them to eat in a restaurant where the food wasn't kosher.

Halfway through the meal David brought Donald Trump's name up. He defended Trump's decision to move the US embassy from Tel Aviv to Jerusalem saying that nothing else mattered as long as his support for Israel remained strong. He mentioned something about American evangelicals believing that the creation of Israel in 1948 was a fulfilment of biblical prophecy that would bring about Christ's return. That comment went straight over my head like a Mitchell Starc bouncer and infuriated the shiska at the table.

"You're saying that his attacks on the media, his constant lying, his gutting of the EPA, his mocking of the disabled, women and war heroes, his affairs with porn stars and colluding with Russia to fix an election doesn't matter?" Julie asked.

"That's right."

"What does matter?"

"His support of Israel. Nothing else."

"You are out of your fucking mind mate," Julie said getting out of her chair. "Come on Ben. We're not going to have a meal with this arsehole."

I tossed a $20 note on the table and followed Julie towards the door.

"Arsehole? Arsehole? And to think we were going to give you a menorah so you could celebrate Hanukkah properly," David yelled at us.

"I think you know where you can stick your menorah David," Julie hollered back.

Julie was so steamed I had to break into a trot to catch up with her.

"Wow," I told her. "I couldn't have said it better myself."

"You're not angry?"

"Angry? Are you kidding? I'm thrilled. We can celebrate Hanukkah by ourselves."

"One thing though, this menorah he spoke of. What is it?"

"It's like a candelabra. It holds eight candles and on each of Hanukkah's eight nights you light one."

"Do we exchange gifts?"

"We could. What would you like?"

"To see Trump impeached."

"Jail to the chief," I chanted.

Julie joined in. "Jail to the chief, jail to the chief."

We sang all the way home. The singing stopped when we opened the door to our backyard.

In less than two hours our puppy had chewed the chairs of our new outdoor dining set to bits.

"Jail for the dog, jail for the dog," I loudly sang.

This time Julie did not join in.

"Knock it off Pavarotti and help me clean this mess up," she said. "Maybe we can get new cushions."

"That may be difficult and expensive," I said.

"Why?"

"I read this morning that Trump was putting a tariff on Australian steel and we've retaliated by putting a tariff on outdoor furniture coming from the states."

"I hate that fucker," she said.

Sick Puppy

My better half and I were out of the house for less than an hour last Saturday. On our way out, we gave our nearly 11-month-old labrador a frozen bone which had more meat on it than an election-day sausage. She had been left on her own numerous times before – and for much longer than an hour – without any serious consequences.

We wished our local candidate good luck on our way toward the voting booths – turned out she needed a lot more than just luck to hold her seat – visited a local garage sale where we walked away empty-handed and walked down to the local watering hole/TAB where I placed a bet on the Doomben Cup – a winner.

We figured the bone would keep the dog's attention for at least half an hour and would be followed by a nap on the newly mown backyard grass in the warm autumnal sunshine.

How wrong we were.

Without any closed-circuit footage to verify her movements, we put on our white CSI-issued lab coats and did our best to recreate the crime scene we returned to. The remnants of the bone were found on the grass outside. She had then come back inside – via the doggy door. We checked the paw prints, they were hers. Judging by the debris field of torn and shredded pages – inside and out – she had grabbed a book and torn it to pieces. There were two books within reach. Foolishly they had been left on the knee-high coffee table. One was from the local library and the other had been purchased two days earlier for a gold coin at the op shop. TAKE A GUESS WHICH ONE SHE RIPPED TO SHREDS?

"No, I'm not kidding. The dog ate a book I borrowed. That's right, she ate it," I explained to the head librarian early the following week.

"You do know you're responsible for replacing the book, don't you," she said.

I looked at her young face, which was framed by a pair of large stylish glasses and determined she might be receptive to a trade.

"What if I gave you a book, one you do not have, and we call it even?"

"What do you have?" she asked.

It was like trading footy cards when I was a kid. "C'mon mate, two Kevin Bartletts for one Ted Whitten? You're dreaming."

"I have Bob Woodward's *Fear.*"

"Hmmm," she said.

"And wait, there's more," I said, sounding like a TV pitchman.

"If you act now, I'll toss in Andrew Rule's *Winx*. What do you say? Do we have a deal?"

"Woodward and Rule for a Carl Hiaasen? I think we can do that. Got the books with you?"

"They're in the car."

"Meet me at the front door in five minutes. Not a word of this to anyone, or the deal's off, got it?"

Just like that, I was in a Martin Scorsese film.

I quickly walked back to the car and saw I had 22 minutes left on the parking meter to complete the transaction.

I grabbed *Fear* and *Winx*, put them in a brown paper bag and waited by the front door half expecting Joe Pesci to show up to close the deal.

"They're in good condition, aren't they?" the librarian asked before taking possession of the two bestsellers.

"Mint."

"Make yourself scarce," she said as she took the bag. She had a brief look around and briskly walked back inside. I was long gone before she sat down at her desk. She erased the Hiaasen book, *Sick Puppy*, the only book by the prolific south Floridian the library had in stock, from its system and entered the information for *Fear* and *Winx* into it. A nearby printer belched out a couple of stickers. She slapped the stickers on the books, inserted a security card into each and put them in their respective places on the shelves.

Late that day I noticed pages of *Sick Puppy* mixed in with our dog's poo. Several times over my long and undistinguished career in journalism, editors had accused me of handing in work that was shit. Right in front of me was a prime example of shitty writing. "See, I told myself, I'm not the only one who writes shit."

I immediately realised my faux pas. You see, In the long history of literature, the words shit, and Hiaasen have appeared in the same sentence just once; in a report by his gastroenterologist summarising a colonoscopy. I immediately emailed Mr Hiaasen to apologise. I'm still waiting for a reply.

We took our dog to the vet first thing in the morning.

"Do you have a garden hose at home," the vet asked.

"We do, why do you ask?"

"Well, the pages of the book made it through the dog's digestive system, without a problem," the vet said. "We're waiting on the cover."

Rock 'n
Rant

A fter a tumultuous couple of years, which included losing his job, his girlfriend, his lifesavings, another girlfriend and half his marbles, which he blamed on the oppressive heat and humidity of Cairns, Gary Delaney had seemingly found happiness in the arms of girlfriend Sue Paice and the glamorous lifestyle the city of Noosa offered.

He lived in Paice's paid-up apartment on glitzy Hastings Street, enjoyed as much sex as his near 60-year-old pecker could handle, played golf twice a week on a championship course without the danger of encountering a sunbaking crocodile, and for the first time since leaving Melbourne nearly three years ago, felt content and settled. Or was he? "To tell you the truth, I'm a bit worried," he told 70-year-old Chuck O'Rourke, over a beer after the two had played 18 holes at Noosa Country Club on a sunny and still Wednesday morning. Delaney couldn't hit a fairway on the front nine and shot a 102, or 10 strokes over his average of 92.

O'Rourke, a noted gambler on and off the course, shot an 89 and was drinking Great Northerns, courtesy of Delaney, who was smart enough to limit his gambling with O'Rourke to a couple of beers.

"What about?" O'Rourke asked.

"Things are going well. Too well. I'm afraid something is going to come along and screw things up."

"Like what?"

"I don't know exactly. Good things never seem to last with me. I'm always expecting disappointment."

"Here? In Noosa? What the hell could possibly go wrong here? The sun doesn't shine for a few days? The tennis courts are off limits for a week because they're being re-surfaced? The pool closes for 48 hours for cleaning? This is heaven my friend. You know how many men your age would give their left nut, and maybe even their right, to have the set-up you do. You're living the dream. Enjoy it."

"I guess you're right," Delaney said.

"What about that racehorse of yours? What was his name again?"

"Too Hard Wrong Spot."

"That's it. Best name ever to get past the stewards."

"We've had to retire him. He did a ligament at trackwork a week ago. And since he's a gelding there'll be no stud fees coming our way."

"Ouch."

"You got that right."

"Going to get involved with another horse?"

"Nah. I had a good run, made some money, had a blast. I'd rather go out a winner."

"You are mate. Just keep your chin up."

Delaney raised his glass and downed the rest of his beer.

The two other members of their foursome, Dick "Sand Trap" Harlow and Billy "No Neck" Farrell, had texted their apologies the night before owing to a doctor's appointment (Harlow) and a routine trip to the dentist (Farrell). No Neck had been complaining about his new dentures the last time the foursome teed off, and on O'Rourke's recommendation, agreed to see his dentist, Harley McGee.

"And you better not cancel. I had to pull a few strings to get you in. He's got a waiting list longer than Delaney's pecker", O'Rourke told

Farrell. "See these," he said pointing to his own choppers, which were whiter than an Arizona Country Club.

"A check-up and a cleaning every six months."

"I won't cancel," Farrell said.

And he didn't, which was why it was just Delaney and O'Rourke enjoying their beers and lunches at an outside table under the welcome shade of a massive umbrella.

"Another salad?" Delaney asked as he dug into a rather large hamburger with the lot.

"Yup. How do you think I look this good at 70?"

Delaney had to admit O'Rourke looked more like he was 60 than 70.

"Healthy living my friend. Nutritious meals, going easy on the beers, an 18-hole walk twice a week and a healthy sex life."

"When will I meet this wife of yours? You talk about her, but I've never seen her, not even a photo. Is she as hot as Sue?"

"Sue's a looker alright, but one look at Mrs O'Rourke and you can toss away those blue pills I hear you need."

Delaney laughed, took another bite of his burger, and dipped several chips into a healthy side of tomato sauce.

"C'mon mate. One photo. That's not too much to ask, is it?"

"I guess not."

O'Rourke took his wallet from his back pocket, not his phone, and flicked through it for a moment until he found what he was looking for. It was a photo of the couple taken at a work function 18 months ago to celebrate O'Rourke's retirement from a front-office job with Cricket New South Wales. He handed it to Delaney, who put down his burger and wiped his hands on the cloth napkin which rested on his lap.

Delaney looked at it and looked at it some more.

"Well?" O'Rourke asked.

"Does she have a sister?"

O'Rourke laughed so hard that several croutons left his mouth and flew in Delaney's direction.

Delaney handed the photo back and nodded.

"I am in the presence of greatness. No wonder I never see you outside of the club. You've got a permanent 'Do not disturb' sign hanging on your front door."

The two said their goodbyes after lunch. Delaney hopped in his Toyota and O'Rourke, all 190 centimetres of him, settled comfortably into a late-model Jaguar and sped off. They'd be back at the club on Sunday morning for their 7am tee time, along with Farrell and Harlow.

None of their wives, or in Delaney's case, his girlfriend, minded. They were fast asleep when their partners approached the first tee.

However, Dick "Sand Trap" Harlow, was nearly a no-show due to an incident on the driving range on Friday afternoon which earned him a reprimand from the country club's top administrator.

Harlow was hitting a bucket of balls to prepare for Sunday's outing when he got into a scuffle with another member.

Rod Mayer had wrongfully accused Harlow of having an affair with his wife, a tall blonde drink of water, who could stop traffic when crossing Hastings Street and make male pedestrians momentarily forget where they were going or why.

Harlow took a moment and said, "I thought about it, but the line was too long."

Mayer lunged at Harlow but got his foot stuck in Harlow's near-empty bucket of balls. They tumbled onto the ground. Both got in several good licks until the scuffle was broken up by other golfers. Mayer and Harlow were both placed on report by the official manning the driving range. They were sent to the main office, where the top dogs wore suits and ties, and whose portraits lined the hallways. Mayer and

Harlow were forced – under the threat of suspension – to apologise to each other, which they begrudgingly did.

"You haven't heard the last of this," Mayer said as the two left club president Whitey Brookline's office.

"I bet I have," Harlow said as he knocked Mayer out of his way with a shoulder charge that Wayne Bennett would have been proud of.

Despite feeling a bit low, Delaney was enjoying a good run of health. All he needed were a couple of prescriptions; one for his slightly elevated blood pressure and another for his borderline cholesterol.

He tried making an appointment with a local GP but was told by a receptionist that the only appointments available at present were telehealth appointments. He made one. It was for the following Tuesday at 11.30am. His details were confirmed which included his date of birth, Medicare number, address, phone number and email address. He was also asked for his credit card number since there was a charge for the telehealth call – $89. The same price as an office visit.

"Eighty-nine dollars? For a phone call?"

"That's correct sir, unless you have a concession card."

"I don't."

"Then you'll be billed $89. You will however receive $51 back from Medicare."

On the Monday, Delaney received a text message to remind him of his telehealth appointment the next day at 11:30am. Respond Yes to confirm or No to cancel. Not cancelling 24 hours before your appointment could incur a fee.

Delaney responded with a Yes.

The next morning, after breakfast with Sue, he went for his morning walk to get his newspaper. His options were the Murdoch paper, the other

Murdoch paper, or the other Murdoch paper. Begrudgingly he bought Murdoch's Brisbane paper. Several months ago, he had asked the owner of the shop to give him at least a day's break from Murdoch's papers and stock the *Saturday Age* from Melbourne. Since so many Melburnians vacationed or spent long weekends it made good sense he said.

The owner agreed. It cost Delaney a tenner each Saturday, but it was money well spent. He spent much of the day reading each section from cover to cover while watching the races and helping Sue tidy up her two-bedroom, two-bathroom unit.

The following Monday morning, Delaney set off on his 15-minute walk to get his newspaper. He crossed busy Hastings Street and was nearly clipped by a car which ran a red light. A furious Delaney threw his hands up, glared at the middle-aged driver and banged on the car's bonnet. "I'm walking here," he yelled, mimicking Dustin Hoffman in the 1969 film *Midnight Cowboy.*

"What the fuck?" Delaney barked as he continued crossing the street. "The bastard never even said sorry. Whatever happened to giving way to pedestrians and not running a red light?"

As he got to the curb, he realised that he should have gotten the number plate of the vehicle. It was too late now.

Delaney bought his paper, walked back home, and started to wait for his telecall. Sue gave Delaney a kiss on her way out. He golfed, she played lawn bowls in an over 55 competition and was quite good at it.

Delaney had his notes in order and his phone fully charged as he waited for the telehealth call with a Dr Jenkins.

Delaney kept one eye on a clock hanging in the kitchen as he read his paper. It ticked over to 11:30. Nothing. Then 11:45. Still nothing.

Maybe he's with a patient or on another call. These things happen, he thought.

With the big hand and little hand now both on the 12, Delaney started to get a bit anxious. 12:15 came and went, nothing. Then 12:30, 1pm.

Maybe he's out to lunch, that's it. He'll call when he gets back.

Now it's 1:30, then 2pm, 3pm. Nothing. Bupkus. Zilch. Nada.

"I'm waiting here. How long I gotta wait?" he yelled at the clock.

By 4pm Delaney gave up. However, he still held on to a glimmer of hope. That maybe the doctor's last call of the day would be to him. It wasn't. Was there a text message, an email, or a phone call from someone at the practice to apologise to him? No.

At 5pm it was clear that there would be no telehealth phone call. He rang the office only to be told to book in another time.

"And what if he doesn't call then?" Delaney asked.

"Dr Jenkins always keeps his telehealth appointments," he was told.

"Well, he didn't keep it on Tuesday."

"Would you like to book another appointment?"

"Yes," he answered.

"The doctor has an opening this coming Tuesday at 11:30. Is that suitable?"

"Yes. I await his call," Delaney said.

He went to hang up only he had been hung up on first.

"WHY IS IT THAT WE GET CHARGED IF WE DO NOT CANCEL AN APPOINTMENT WITHIN 24 HOURS?" Delaney yelled.

"I SHOULD SEND HIS OFFICE AN INVOICE FOR WASTING MY TIME TODAY. THEY SHOULD HAVE TOLD ME DAMN IT."

"What's with all the yelling?" Sue asked when she got home. "I heard you coming out of the lift."

"I had that telehealth call today but the doctor never called. Nor did anyone from his office. No text message, no email. Nothing. I would love to send them an invoice for wasting my time today."

"You should. Give then a taste of their own medicine."

"I just might. He gets one more chance. Next Tuesday at 11:30. If there's no call, he gets an invoice."

The call came just on the stroke of 11:30. Delaney got his scripts and didn't tee off on Dr Jenkins because the doctor was so damn nice and accommodating.

Delaney's twice-weekly golf outings and almost daily lunches with Sue at the Noosa Surf Lifesaving Club always gave him a lift, but he wanted more. Not from Sue, she was the ideal partner. He missed going to an office five days a week and kibbitzing with his colleagues. He decided to bring it up with Sue one evening as they watched the sun go down from her balcony.

Sue understood and offered nothing but encouragement.

"What else would you like to do Gary?"

"I may have mentioned before that I did some radio work back in the day."

Sue nodded. "You did. And you enjoyed it."

He still did an occasional racing segment for a Melbourne station, offering insight as a part-owner of a former Melbourne Cup contender and giving the occasional tip.

"I was driving home from the club the other afternoon, turned on the radio and could not believe the garbage I heard.

The presenters were dull, lifeless, and just plain boring. The music was just as bad. I was better as a 19-year-old at the uni radio station I volunteered at. I played Zeppelin, Pink Floyd, The Beatles. We all had a blast and talked about shit that we got up to over the weekend, the footy, our girlfriends – if we had one – and what we were going to do when we graduated. Geez, I miss those days."

Sue refreshed her drink and told her partner to go down to the local station and have a talk to the people in charge.

"Maybe they could find a place for you. You've got nothing to lose."

Delaney agreed. He thanked Sue for her encouragement and two mornings later showed up at HOT105.5 FM unannounced.

He asked the receptionist if he could see Lou Watson, the station's program director. The station's website had bios and photos of all the presenters and station management.

"Who shall I say is here?" the perky young receptionist asked.

"Howard Stern."

She punched a few digits into her phone and said, "a Mr Howard Stern is here to see you, Lou."

Delaney heard Lou's laughter through the receptionist's headset. "Send him in."

Delaney walked down a long corridor and said hello to several people informally gathered around a large conference room table. He guessed they were ad reps. The door to Watson's office was open. He knocked.

Watson got up from behind his desk, walked over to Delaney and with a wide smile on his face said, "a real pleasure to meet you, Howard. Come in, take a seat. You don't have as much hair as I remembered."

"Marriage will do that to you Lou. As soon as the divorce papers are served the hair starts falling out."

"Tell me about it," Watson said as he ran a hand over his thinning brown hair.

"So, what brings the King of All Media to Noosa. Had enough of New York?"

Delaney laughed. "Never been, but I do watch and listen to the highlights of his show on YouTube."

"If only I had someone with a third of his talent I'd be on easy street."

"You're looking at him," Delaney said.

Watson laughed. A racing tragic, he said, "You're Gary Delaney, aren't you? One of the owners of Too Hard Wrong Spot?"

"In the flesh."

"What brings you to Noosa?"

"A Toyota RAV4, but I left it in the parking lot."

Watson let loose with a laugh and banged a hand on his desk which rattled the coffee mug sitting on it.

"What can I do for you Gary?"

"I'll be blunt. I'm retired and I'm looking for something to do besides play golf and shtup my lady friend. You can take one of those lifeless turds you have polluting the airwaves off and put me on instead."

"You're serious?"

"Yup."

"I did radio back at Uni and I do a racing spot on Melbourne radio every couple of weeks."

"Go on."

"I'm gonna make you an offer you can't refuse. I'll work the first month for free. Once the ad money starts pouring in, you can pay me. And if it doesn't, I'll walk."

Watson looked at the large whiteboard behind his desk which had the station's line-up on it. There wasn't a single empty space. He pointed to Saturday and Sunday.

"We run syndicated crap on Saturday and Sunday nights from 8pm to midnight. Then the station computer takes over until 6am when our live breakfast show comes on. The brekkie show runs seven days a week. Presenters don't mind getting up early, but they hate late nights."

"I'm just the opposite," Delaney said.

"So, what would you do if I put you on air? And that's a big if."

Delaney was well prepared for the question.

"I'll talk some sport, go over the Saturday and Sunday AFL and NRL games, review the weekend's feature races, have a few laughs, talk about things that bug me, have a look at the front page of the paper, and play some good old-fashioned rock 'n roll. The show will be called Rock 'n Rant."

He told Watson how he was almost cleaned up when he went for his daily newspaper and about his telehealth call where he waited and waited and waited. Watson nodded his head and seemed to like what he heard.

"I'll tell you what Gary. I'm filling in for our afternoon guy on Friday. He's got a wedding in Sydney he's going to. Come in and do the show with me. Do one or two of your rants and pick the music. If we get a good response, I'll put you on Saturday and Sunday nights. You've got to learn how to use the board though and view some videos that human resources insist we all watch."

"I'm a quick learner," Delaney lied.

"Come in around 3:30. I'll introduce you after the 4pm news. You do the weather, and we'll chat in between the music. What do you say Howard?"

"I'll be here. Thank you," Delaney said as he shook Watson's hand.

"See Denise at reception. She'll give you some paperwork you'll need to fill out."

"Will do."

Delaney couldn't wait to get home and tell Sue the good news.

We'll have a night out. I'm so glad she gave me the nudge I needed to go down there.

Sue was so pleased to hear the news that she dressed up as a flight attendant for him after dinner.

"Are you a member of the mile-high club sir?" she asked seductively while she positioned herself on Delaney's lap.

"I am now. I love this airline," he yelled.

Delaney wrote down a few bits over the next day and a half and brought Murdoch's Brisbane paper to the station with him on Friday afternoon.

"Hi Howard, nice to see you again," the receptionist said as he walked into the building. Delaney laughed at the now running gag. *Should I tell her?* he thought. *Nah, let's see how long it takes before she catches on.*

Mr Watson is expecting you, he's in studio 1. Up the stairs and on your right."

"Thank you. I don't believe we've been formally introduced. Your name is?"

"Savannah. Savannah Whitney."

Had he had a hat with him, Delaney would have doffed it in her direction before climbing up the short flight of stairs.

"Nice to make your acquaintance Savannah."

The door to Studio 1 was closed, and the red *On Air* sign was lit. Watson waved as he read some ad copy and when he was done motioned for Delaney to come in.

Watson was seated behind a mass of screens and had two control boards in front of him which he worked effortlessly.

Fuck, I might be over my head here, Delaney thought.

As Gerry Rafferty's 'Baker Street' played through a pair of large speakers mounted to the left and right of him, Watson motioned for Delaney to sit down in the chair across from him. He adjusted a microphone and placed it in front of Delaney.

"Do you want a pair of headphones?"

"Not necessary."

"The 4pm news airs after Rafferty. I'll read the sport and then throw it over to you for the weather. For the rest of this afternoon and evening. The weekend's forecast. That sort of thing. Ad lib all you like.

"Then I'll lead you into that dust-up you had with the driver who ran that red light. Get fired up. I reckon the listeners will eat that up. And later tell us about how you waited and waited for that telehealth call. It's Rock 'n Rant, right?"

"It is. Tell me something Lou, have you worked for NASA? Look at that freaking board in front of you."

"You'll pick it up in a couple of years," Watson joked.

Delaney was supposed to be on the air with Watson for just an hour, but the two hit it off so well, that Watson asked him to stay until the show wrapped up at 6pm.

"Savannah says the phone downstairs hasn't stopped ringing and two of the sales guys texted me asking when you were coming back on air."

"No shit?"

"No shit. Keep your Saturday and Sunday nights clear. As soon as you learn how to use this board, you're going on. I'll have one of our tech guys train you during the week if that's okay with you. For those first couple of shows somebody will be sitting next to you in case anything goes wrong. The one thing we don't want is dead air."

Delaney came in for his training two days a week over the next two weeks and took notes, notes, and more notes. In addition to the station's operating manual, Delaney had more than a dozen pages of hand-written notes, several of which he was able to read.

The station ran several smart promos for Delaney's new show in the week leading up to his debut. He was impressed with their quality. The tagline, played over Zeppelin's classic 'Rock and Roll', was ... *We're Making Radio Great Again. Rock 'n Rant from 8pm this Saturday and Sunday.*

Delaney and Sue had an early dinner that first Saturday. He asked Sue to come along for some moral support and she agreed. She had a great laugh and if she laughed – or even smiled at what he was saying – he knew he was hitting the right notes.

Joe Shields, the same tech man who taught Delaney how to run the board, was by his side. And Delaney was glad he was. There was a second of dead air here and there when Delaney went to a commercial break or when he went to a tune after one of his rants.

"You're doing well mate. Another few shows and you'll be on your own. And I'll be just a phone call away if anything goes wrong."

Sue Paice knew more about computers, programming, and apps than anyone Delaney knew. She stood behind him and Shields during the second hour, scribbled down a few notes and told Delaney during an ad break that the system was user friendly, whatever the hell that meant.

Delaney started running out of gas by hour number three. Shields started rubbing his eyes and Sue was asleep in her chair across from him. By the time he signed off just before midnight, he was mentally exhausted but on a high.

I wonder what Watson thought of the show, he wondered.

He found out the next afternoon when the program director texted him.

"Great debut mate. Loved the show. Good luck tonight."

"Tonight? Holy shit. I better start preparing. He read the Sunday paper and checked a few odd news sites. There was nothing better for odds news than the ultra-conservative *New York Post*, another horse in Murdoch's stable. The tabloid focused on celebrity nonsense, crime, and took pride in denigrating anything President Biden and the Democratic Party did, even though their policies helped many of its readers.

Delaney filled several pages of a yellow legal pad with numerous notes and jotted down the scores of that day's AFL and NRL games before he went on air at 8:05pm.

Shields was again at his side and Sue accompanied Delaney to the studio for the second straight night although this time it took a bit more urging.

"You don't need me there Gary. I don't want to get home at 12:30 in the morning. Joe will make sure everything runs smoothly."

"He will but I'm afraid if you're not there I'll stumble a bit, my good luck will run out. How about coming along just for the first hour? We'll ring for an Uber to take you home. Deal?"

"Deal."

Sue and Delaney arrived at 7:30. Shields let them into the building and while he and Delaney worked on the night's rundown sheet and music, Sue sat in the same chair as the previous night, took out a book and started to read like so many wives and girlfriends of local cricketers do on Saturday afternoons. But she closed it whenever Delaney spoke on air.

He occasionally heard her laugh through his headphones which spurred him on.

Two weeks later Delaney was doing the show on his own. It wasn't as much fun without someone in the studio. But the phone calls, 90 per cent of which were positive, provided him with a bit of company. The other 10 per cent didn't like his taste in music.

What the heck is wrong with Zeppelin, Pink Floyd, Tom Petty, The Stones, The Beatles, The Eagles, Fleetwood Mac? he asked himself. *I'm not going to play songs we've all heard a thousand times.*

He did take one caller's advice and played lighter fare after 10pm. Delaney conceded the caller had a valid point. Nobody wanted to hear *Black Dog* at 11:15 at night.

The tunes became less frequent as Delaney talked more about his personal life; aging, the frequent night-time trips to the toilet, his hassles with apps and doing everything online and his golf game.

He ranted about people taking up two parking spots at a shopping centre, people who did not return trollies to their proper collection point when they went to Woolies or Coles. He got stuck into the Murdoch papers and on occasion had a few unflattering things to say about the local council. "I may be wrong, but that's my opinion," he'd say.

To give the show a boost, Delaney took an ad out in the local weekly Noosa newspaper to promote the show. The $500 was well worth it. While the Saturday and Sunday nighttime slots weren't included in the ratings, Watson knew he had a winner due to the demand for spots. The Joke of the Day segment on the stroke of midnight became so popular that the sales team found a mattress store to sponsor it. The perfect fit.

Eventually every segment had a sponsor, and it was new money. The syndicated programs that Delaney replaced brought in peanuts. The Rock 'n Rant show was substantially adding to the station's bottom line and Delaney knew it. He had the upper hand when he and Watson sat down one Friday afternoon to talk money.

"Throw out a number Gary," Watson said.

"Three hundred and fifty dollars per shift," he replied.

Watson held out his hand. Delaney shook it.

"I'll have our office manager draw up a contract. Keep the amount to yourself, okay? You're the highest paid presenter on the staff, and you deserve to be."

"Deal."

"What was that joke you told last Sunday? The one with Little Johnny?"

A smile crossed Delaney's face. He leaned back in his chair and said ...

"Little Johnny is sitting on a park bench munching on his sixth candy bar of the afternoon.

An older man on the bench across from him says, 'Son, you know eating all that candy isn't good for you. It will give you acne, rot your teeth and make you fat.' Little Johnny replied, 'My grandfather lived to be 107 years old.' The man asked, 'Did your grandfather eat six candy bars at a time?' 'No, he minded his own fucking business!'"

Watson laughed so hard he had tears in his eyes.

"Keep 'em coming," he said.

Delaney had been living on his savings, what was left of his super and the court settlement he received in Cairns when his former financial advisor turned girlfriend got sent to jail for stealing from him and several other clients. He was still a few years away from receiving the aged pension.

Even though he wasn't paying Sue any rent, he did pay the electric, internet and water bills, and picked up most of the checks when they went out to lunch and dinner, so the extra money came in handy.

After his successful meeting with Watson, Delaney stopped at a florist for a dozen red roses and then a chemist where he bought a bottle of Sue's favourite perfume. He didn't remember the name but recognised the bottle.

"For your encouragement, support, and love," he wrote on the card that came with the roses.

Sue was overwhelmed by Gary's thoughtfulness, and they celebrated his good fortune with dinner at a seafood restaurant overlooking the Noosa River and again when they got home. They tumbled into bed and were enjoying each other when Delaney suddenly got up and walked out of the bedroom with just his socks on.

"Where are you going?"

Delaney looked over his shoulder and asked, "do we have any of that strawberry sauce left"?

"Second shelf in the pantry, left-hand side."

Football season came and went. Penrith and Sydney won the NRL and AFL premierships, respectively, which meant it was time for Delaney's favourite time of the year, the spring racing carnival.

Delaney previewed the lead-up races to the Caufield and Melbourne Cups and the Cox Plate and interviewed several trainers and jockeys on air. He nailed the winner of the Cox Plate, a European invader, and on Cup Day took Sue out for lunch at their favourite spot, the Noosa Surf Lifesaving Club.

Had there been a Fashions on the Field competition Sue would have finished top three. The 57-year-old brunette looked sensational in a lavender off-the-shoulder dress with a matching fascinator and heels which showed off her great legs.

Delaney wore his favourite blue sports coat, a light blue shirt, beige coloured slacks, and loafers. He would not have figured in the men's division voting.

Among the entries in the 24-horse field was Queensland Derby winner Trinity Beach, which is the suburb Delaney called home when lived he Cairns.

"I've got to back it," he told Sue. "He's 20-1."

Sue's tip was a Melbourne based mare named Golf Widow. It fit considering Delaney spent as much time on the golf course as he did at home.

Delaney went to the crowded TAB counter at the club and tossed $20 to win and place on both horses along with a $20 quinella involving the same two.

With Sue cheering Golf Widow home, the horse won the Cup by a neck over a horse from the UK with Trinity Beach another neck back in third. It was the happiest Delaney had ever seen Sue. She had Delaney snap a photo of her holding the winning ticket before she cashed it.

Golf Widow paid $37.60 for the win and $8.20 the place while Trinity Beach returned $5.20 for running third.

Sue won nearly $900 while Delaney won $10. Better than losing.

A couple of weeks before Christmas, when everyone's spirits were soaring, Delaney showed up at the station for a meeting with Lou Watson. Savannah was at her usual post but had been crying and everyone else was gathered in small groups consoling each other.

What in the wide, wide world of sport is going on here? Delaney wondered.

He asked around and soon got his answer.

Doris Franelli, the station's bookkeeper for the past dozen years, had been stealing money from the station to feed her gambling habit. The numbers weren't all in yet, but it was in the neighbourhood of $350,000.

"We're bankrupt," a shaken Watson told Delaney in his office. "She cooked the books. We'll never get that money back. We're closing our doors at the end of the week. There's no other way out. The company doesn't have that sort of cash on hand. It's Christmas for goodness' sake. What am I going to tell my wife and kids?"

"What's happened to Doris," Delaney asked.

"She was taken out of here in handcuffs first thing this morning. The local paper was tipped off. This will be all over the news tonight. We are totally fucked."

"Maybe not," Delaney said.

"What do you mean?"

"I know a couple of guys in Melbourne who might want to diversify."

"A couple of guys? Who are they?"

"This goes no further, understand?"

Watson nodded.

"Two big-time gamblers, and I mean big time, Johnny Pastrami and Frankie Fingers Tannenbaum. Sit tight. I'll talk to them and if they like the idea, their lawyer will call you later this afternoon. However, there may be a condition or two attached."

Watson's shoulders sank.

"Pastrami's girlfriend has always wanted to be on the air."

"Can she put two words together? Does she know who *The Beatles* are?"

"Yes and no."

"Oh boy."

"Don't worry Lou. I'll coach her."

"We each like a bet Gary. What are the odds of Pastrami and the other fellow bailing us out?"

"About $1.75. Leave it with me."

Delaney looked at his watch. It was 11:10am.

"You'll have an answer by 5pm this afternoon."

Watson got out of his chair and gave Delaney a bear hug.

"You get us out of this mess, and you can have the morning slot."

"I don't do mornings Lou. But a raise couldn't hurt."

"Five hundred a shift?"

"Done."

Acknowledgements

As always, special thanks to Kerry Russell, Simon McEvoy, David Turner, Brad Beitzel, Chris Tatman, Professor Quincy Adams Wagstaff, Dr Hugo Z Hackenbush, Stan the Caddie, Triumph, the Insult Comic Dog, Rex the kelpie, Bernie the 40kg labrador/chicken parmigiana cross for not eating the manuscript, the fine folks at Cairns FM 89.1 and ... the Forty South team of Lucinda Sharp, Kent Whitmore and Rayne Allinson for their support, suggestions, and encouragement.

Marty Shevelove
Tasmania, May 2024

www.ingramcontent.com/pod-product-compliance
Lightning Source LLC
Chambersburg PA
CBHW030625120726
47904CB00006B/2035